MW01697458

CATRIONA'S WAR

JEAN GRAINGER

GOLD HARP MEDIA

Copyright © 2023 by GOLD HARP MEDIA

All rights reserved.

No part of this book may be reproduced in any form or by any electronic or mechanical means, including information storage and retrieval systems, without written permission from the author, except for the use of brief quotations in a book review.

❀ Created with Vellum

CHAPTER 1

October, 1938. Eupen, Belgium

'Au revoir, Catriona, bonne chance, et que Dieu te bénisse.' The Mother Superior of Lycée Sainte Yvette de Huy insisted on kissing Catriona on both cheeks – brushing dry, crusty lips across her skin. Catriona steeled herself not to flinch.

'Je vous remercie, ma bonne soeur,' she whispered, eyes downcast, as the nuns had taught her.

Her father had already carried her luggage to his car, thanked the nun, and now he was waiting for her, his hand resting on the passenger door. Following him, she climbed into the open-topped MG, careful not to shock the watching nun by revealing a glimpse of knee. Kieran McCarthy walked around to the other side, lowered himself into the driver's seat, started the engine and drove away down the long, sunlit avenue.

Catriona didn't once look back at the red-bricked convent boarding school that had been her home for so long.

She was eighteen now and her school days were over, yet it wasn't until they had passed through the imposing black wrought-iron gates – topped by an enormous crucifix – that she finally felt able to breathe.

'Well, thank God that's done with.' Uncrossing her legs, she reached into the glove compartment for her father's packet of Gauloises.

Kieran nodded, handing her his precious silver lighter: 'I know. That last half hour was tedious in the extreme.'

She was incredulous at his audacity. 'Are you seriously complaining to me about putting up with that walking corpse for five minutes? I was stuck in there for twelve bloody years. *And* I could have been out of there three months ago if you'd only bothered to collect me before the summer.'

He winked at her. 'Ah Catriona, my pet – you know I have to travel for my work.'

'You don't "have to" anything, Kieran.' She never called him Father or Daddy, as her friends addressed their fathers. To her, he was always just Kieran. She lit two cigarettes, stuck one between his lips, and inhaled gratefully the other one herself, then settled back into her seat, blowing out a long blue line of smoke. 'You don't *have* to be a foreign correspondent for Reuters. You could choose to go back to being a home reporter for the Irish Times.'

'But that would be no fun.'

'Fun?' Her eyes flashed. 'It's only *you* who's been having fun while I've been stuck here with those awful nuns, with all their praying and their stupid rules.'

'Ah Catriona, I brought you home with me to Dublin every summer…'

'For a few weeks and then you'd rush off again!'

'But at least you weren't too far from your Uncle Gaston, and Mémé and Pépé in Saint-Émilion…'

'But this summer Mémé and Pépé retired and Uncle Gaston had to take over the chateau and vineyard. So everyone was far too busy to be bothered with me, and I've been trapped in that prison without a break.'

He grinned. *'Prison?'*

She scowled. 'Yes, prison. The nuns were *horrible*. If they caught me speaking *"en anglais"* they went mad altogether. Herr Paasch taught maths in German and I'm bad enough at maths anyway without having to figure out his awful Hamburg accent, and Frau Moller, a total beast of a woman, tried to teach me deportment but I was terrible at it. She told me I was the wrong shape, too big on top and legs like a heron. I was always falling over my own feet.'

Kieran McCarthy was laughing as he drove.

Catriona glared at him. 'It's not funny! I was always in trouble, constantly punished, while you were living it up in hotels around the world. And the postcards only made it worse let me tell you, in case they were to salve your conscience.'

Crossly, she turned to the window, undoing the top buttons on her tight school blouse and pulling off the regulation navy blue ribbon that kept her silky blonde locks in check. She shook out her hair, loosening it in the autumn breeze.

'Catriona…' He gave her a playful nudge.

'Shh. Don't talk to me. I'm being angry with you.' She was only mock disgruntled though, and he knew it. It hadn't been that bad: she'd made good friends like Margot and Trudi, and at least on most holidays she'd got to visit her grandparents Louise and Philippe de Clairand in the chateau, and her mother's brother Gaston and his lovely little family.

As the car sped on down the tree-lined roads, she realised she was still clutching his beloved silver lighter in her hand.

Turning it over, she read the inscription for the thousandth time.

Car, vois-tu, chaque jour je t'aime daventage, aujourd'hui plus qu'hier et bien moins que demain.

Ton Amour, Eloise

How often she'd read those words, as a child:

Because, you see, each day I love you more, today more than yesterday, and less than tomorrow.

Your love, Eloise.

A fleeting glimpse of her mother surfaced in her mind, but failed to solidify and flickered back to nothing. She had always longed for a true lasting memory, but it had eluded her for her whole life. All she knew of her mother was from old black and white photographs, which showed a small, beautiful young woman with an hourglass figure, very pale hair and dark eyes.

Catriona was conscious of her father gazing at her with a smile, and she knew what he was thinking: the same as he always did when he'd not seen her for a while. He was thinking that she was so much like her mother, it was uncanny, and that she grew more like Eloise every year.

Back in 1920, nineteen-year-old Eloise de Clairand had been studying English in Dublin when – much to the horror of her aristocratic French parents – she had fallen for a young Irish cub reporter and brought him back with her to France. They'd lived together in a tiny apartment in Lyon, where Catriona was born. The scandal of having a baby outside of wedlock was the last straw for Kieran's parents, who hadn't approved of him running off with a strange French girl in the first place. Luckily, the young couple were so in love and so delighted with their new baby girl; they didn't care what their respective families thought. They had each other and that was enough.

Kieran got a job with *Le Progrès*, a Lyonnais newspaper, as their international correspondent, and Eloise – a natural linguist – taught English and cared for their little girl.

Six years later, and married, they decided they could finally afford a honeymoon. They rented a small chalet on the banks of Lake Mirabel. Eloise was a brave swimmer and on the first day, leaving Kieran to mind Catriona, she set out to swim the lake. That evening, her body was found washed up on the far shore, and Kieran McCarthy's halcyon days were over forever.

Six-year-old Catriona's life also changed beyond recognition. Not trusting their son-in-law to bring her with him on his travels, Eloise's parents had insisted on funding a boarding school education for their granddaughter. Since that day, Catriona had been waiting to be old enough to be permanently reunited with her father, and to travel with him to every corner of the globe.

Now that time had come.

'Catriona?'

She smiled to herself. It was hard to pretend to be annoyed with Kieran for very long. He was so handsome and charming – tall, with a warm smile and jet black hair that came to his collar, and such vivid green eyes. Her classmates would swoon over him, on the rare occasions he came to visit. She turned and handed the lighter back to him and he returned it to the pocket of his linen jacket. His wife's last gift was always on his person; it was never thrown carelessly on a table or left in a drawer.

'Are you hungry, pet?' he asked.

Her eyes lit up. 'Did you bring something to eat? Please say you did, the nuns had us all starved at the convent.'

Smiling, he pointed to a paper bag between the seats.

With a cry of joy, she pounced on the patisserie bag, extracted a custard tart and gratefully sank her teeth into it, wiping the crumbs with the back of her hand before digging into the bag again. The girls in school used to marvel at how perfect Catriona's slight curves remained, considering all she ate. Another legacy from her mother, by all accounts.

'So, how's everything at home?' she asked through a mouthful of fresh buttery Madeleine cake. Despite being born in France and growing up in Belgium, she always thought of Ireland as her home. It was her father's country, and therefore hers.

'I've not been back for a while.' He crushed out his cigarette in the car's ashtray. 'I've been in Germany this summer, covering the latest Nazi rally in Nuremberg. They get more elaborate every year. This time it was all about the glorious *Anschluss* between Germany and Austria. They just love him, that Hitler. It's almost a religion, the way they adore him. Still, he's saying all the right things, and Germany was flattened after Versailles so you can kind of see why – but it's weird there now, the Nazis control everything and anyone who has anything negative to say about them...let's just say, it doesn't end well.'

Catriona loved it when her father spoke to her as if she were an adult. She tried to sound knowledgeable. 'I suppose he'll want to take over Belgium next.'

For a while, Kieran remained silent, and she feared she'd said something stupid, but then he answered lightly. 'Who knows? This German-speaking bit of Belgium is probably too insignificant for the Führer.'

She felt relieved. 'And it's not just German-speaking, of course. Everyone here speaks French as well.'

He glanced at her. 'And you?'

'Yes, I'm officially trilingual now,' she acknowledged with a flourish and a grin. 'The nuns made us speak nothing but French. Learning German was harder, but I'm good at languages. Trudi – she's from Frankfurt, remember her? –

says my accent is quite acceptable for a girl educated in Belgium.'

'Ah yes, Trudi. What's she going to do now?'

'Go home to Germany, probably to marry Gerhardt, who wrote to her every week since our first year. He's nice, he came with her parents last summer and they all took Trudi and me out for a picnic on the banks of the Vesdre. They felt sorry for me being virtually an orphan…' She glanced at him mischievously to show she was only joking. 'Anyway, her parents came to collect her in July. I've really missed her since. It's hard to imagine them all as supporters of Hitler but I think they are. Her father works for some official organisation and her little brother is in a thing like the boy scouts except it's all about Hitler apparently. We were kind of sheltered from the world by the nuns but the letters the German girls kept getting from home were a bit eye-opening.'

He looked grim. 'Hitler means business anyway, no doubt about that.'

The German-language road signs and shop fronts were falling behind them as they passed out of this part of Belgium towards Calais in northern France. There, they would catch the ferry to Dover and then drive across England to catch another ferry to Dublin.

'So, back to Dublin and then where?' she asked him, licking the last of the crumbs from her fingers and wiping them on her skirt.

Acting as if he hadn't heard her, he opened up the little MG on the longer, wider road. He drove too hard and fast but she felt safe with him. She would always feel safe with him. Whether he liked it or not, she was determined to travel the world with him, wherever his reporting took them. She was a grown woman now, not a silly little girl who could be left behind.

CHAPTER 2

August, 1940. Dublin

'I'M TWENTY, I'm an adult! If you won't take me with you this time, I don't care; I'm going to London anyway. Dublin is driving me insane. Do you know what I did last week? I'll tell you, shall I? Folded three hundred linen napkins and I only had the pleasure of folding the stupid things after I'd ironed them. No, I've decided. I've had enough of this. I'm coming with you this time and I don't care what you say.'

Catriona wished her voice didn't sound so whiney. When she'd been preparing this conversation in her mind, she'd sounded like an adult. In reality, she found herself on the point of childish tears.

It was all Kieran's fault. Despite her hopes for travelling everywhere with her father, he had constantly refused to take her with him. Instead, he'd made her take a job in the Royal Hotel on Dame Street where she was supposed to be front of house – her ability to converse in three languages being her greatest strength. Yet since the war broke out there were no tourists and she'd been demoted to housekeeping, which she absolutely loathed. Last week she'd had to rebuff the advances of the married and distinctly slimy manager, Mr Kingston, by kneeing him in the balls when he'd cornered her in the stationery cupboard.

She couldn't stick it a moment longer.

She accepted that Kieran felt war-torn Europe was too dangerous for her right now. She hadn't tried to make him take her with him when Reuters sent him to Paris to report on the fall of France to the Nazis. However, his next assignment was in London, and that was where she wanted to be. There was no real war raging in England, there were so many opportunities there, and Margot, her English friend from the convent days, kept on urging her to come over. It was all dances and uniforms and so much fun.

Kieran stood in the sunny kitchen of their two-bedroomed terraced house in Rathgar, rifling through all the post that had come for him in the month he'd been gone and clearly only half-listening to his daughter's rant. He looked more dishevelled than usual – his hair needed to be cut and his clothes were very worn.

She grabbed the letters from him, throwing them on the draining board, her brown eyes flashing with fury. 'I'm speaking to you!' she shouted.

'No, you're not,' her father replied calmly. 'You're roaring at me, an entirely different thing. Now, I'm starving, and since I wouldn't dream of asking if there was anything to eat in this house, I'm going to the Shelbourne for lunch and you are welcome to join me – but the fishwife impression has to stop.' He smiled sweetly at her, which drove her even more mad. However, she knew if she kept on shouting, he would just walk away.

'Fine, I'll get my coat.' She turned on her heel, seething internally.

When she returned to the kitchen, she saw him wince as he stretched to put the bills on the shelf.

'What's wrong?' she cried in alarm – her anger forgotten. 'Are you hurt?'

He became evasive. 'No, I'm fine, had a few too many drinks one night and fell down the stairs.'

'Show me,' she demanded, pulling open his shirt. To her horror, his entire chest was black and blue; the skin grazed and cut. 'You never got all that just falling downstairs! Tell me the truth!'

He shrugged, doing up the buttons again. 'Fine. I was in the wrong place with the wrong woman and her husband had something to say about it. Now, stop fussing. Are we going to eat or not?' He kissed the top of her head and ushered her out the door. Clearly, he was in no mood to discuss it further.

All the way to St Stephen's Green, she kept her hand tucked into his arm. She hated the idea of him getting into such scrapes – she knew nobody would ever replace her mother in his heart, but she'd seen how women flirted with him and he clearly needed Catriona to keep him on the straight and narrow.

The Horseshoe Bar in the Shelbourne was thronged. Several people recognised Kieran from the pieces he regularly contributed to the Irish Times. His articles were syndicated wherever a free press remained. Some came up to speak to him, asking his opinion about what was going on in Europe. He was as open and honest in his answers as he was in his journalism, but he wound up the conversations quickly and then gave his daughter his full attention.

'Now, tell me calmly what you have in mind and we can

talk about it like rational adults.' He ordered a bottle of claret and poured each of them a glass.

Catriona took a deep breath. 'Please let me come with you to London, Kieran.'

He sighed. 'Is it really that bad here that you want to leave neutral Ireland to live in a country which is at war?'

'I'm sorry, but I just hate it here. I know I'm Irish and all of that, and you are too, and we'll always be Irish in our hearts, but I've been away so long, and I don't feel like I fit in anymore. I loved Ireland when I was a child because it was always time with you and we did lots of great things together, but now, here on my own, I feel like a stranger. I'll never make real friends. The girls at the hotel think I'm a snob because I use French words by accident. The food is horrible and everywhere feels so *small*... If I were in London with you, at least I wouldn't feel so alone.'

He looked sad. 'I'm sorry you're so unhappy in Dublin, my pet. It's a shame you can't go to your mother's family in Saint-Émilion.'

Catriona shook her head. 'I love Mémé and Pépé and Gaston and Marie-Claire, but that's not where I want to be.'

'And even if you wanted to be there, France is too dangerous right now – especially for you.'

She was taken aback. 'Especially for me?'

He smiled wryly. 'You're my daughter, Catriona, and I'm not very popular there, to put it mildly. I've written very bluntly about what I think of Hitler and his henchmen, and about the pitiful capitulation of the French under their jack-boots.' He took a quick mouthful of his wine, although the action of raising his glass to his mouth caused him to wince slightly, then added under his breath, 'The arrogance and naiveté of them – thinking the Maginot Line would save them, and then the chaos when the French government scattered, causing the French army to collapse. *Pétain* is a fool, and worse, a German puppet.'

Catriona shuddered. The idea of Hitler's soldiers ordering her French family about made her blood boil. It seemed wherever Germany set its sights they just marched in and took over, helping themselves to what wasn't theirs… It made her think of slimy Mr Kingston. She played her final card. 'That's another reason you have to take me with you to London. The hotel manager tried to pin me against the wall in the stationery cupboard so I had to knee him in the balls to escape.'

'Did he hurt you?' asked Kieran, suddenly paying close attention.

'No, I'm fine, but men know I'm here on my own and I feel so vulnerable…' This wasn't strictly true. Despite her small size, she was well able to take care of herself and see off unwanted attention. But she had to try everything to win this argument.

Kieran sighed and sat back, fixing his daughter with his steady gaze. She knew that look. It was one of the reasons he was so successful as a journalist: he could sense lies much better than anyone she knew. After what seemed like an hour, he finally spoke: 'Fine. You can come to London.'

She couldn't believe her ears. Was he agreeing to let her travel with him?

'Thank you so much!' she gasped.

He pulled a face – half-humorous, half-exasperated. 'You won't like it, I'm warning you. For one thing, you eat like a horse and if you think the food here is bad, wait until you've tried some serious rationing. I give you six months and you'll be begging to come home...'

'I won't, I promise!'

'…so I won't sell our place, we'll rent it to a woman I know in the embassy looking for a place to live. I'm going back to France for a while next week, provided that my contacts can get me in, although it's getting harder and harder…'

'Oh, I see.' Her heart sunk. He was going again, without her.

'…so how about you travel over to England, stay with your friend Margot and find us a house to rent in London? I'll come and meet you there.'

Catriona grinned from ear to ear. Her father trusted her to find them a house. He must see her as an adult after all.

CHAPTER 3

November, 1940. London

Catriona shivered on the hard wooden bench in the tube station, surrounded by terrified and traumatised Londoners. The pounding of the bombs dropping above them was grating on everyone's already frayed nerves.

She and her father had barely moved into their house in Holborn before the bombing started. For so long everyone had been calling it the Phoney War, but Hitler had only been biding his time. Since the seventh of September, the city had been bombarded. The wail of the air raid sirens, the ominous humming of the German planes, the fire and ambulance bells, they never seemed to stop. The daytime attack of the fifteenth of September had been especially terrifying, but after that, Hitler seemed to restrict the air raids to the hours of darkness.

Kieran McCarthy had made his daughter promise that she'd take shelter in Chancery Lane tube station every time the air raid sirens sounded – even if he wasn't there to make her. And of course, he never was there. She had dreamed of taking such good care of him in London, greeting him at the door every night, serving him the beautiful French cuisine she had learnt to cook at the convent. Instead, she could count on the fingers of one hand the number of nights he'd actually slept in the house she'd found for them.

Even now, he was in America. He'd left in the third week of September, to tour America lecturing about his experiences in Nazi-controlled Europe and urging them to join the war. She was glad he'd gone somewhere safe this time, but she still missed him horribly, and worried for his health. Before he'd left, she'd noticed his articles – so outspoken about the Nazi regime – had become less frequent, and he'd seemed increasingly stressed and harassed. Perhaps he was worried that newspapers no longer wanted his copy.

She herself was now working in the offices of the Daily Express on Lower Thames Street, as a junior copy editor. She longed to be a famous reporter like her father and would have liked him to get her a start higher up the ladder, but he'd only said that he had 'started sweeping the floor of the Irish Press in Dublin and worked my way up, and if you want it badly enough, you'll do the same.'

So she made tea, ran errands and occasionally got to proofread the classifieds where people sold furniture or looked for lost pets. Everyone was preoccupied, and she didn't make any friends. She was the youngest by many years and she was one of only three women – the other two being a pair of sisters that worked in accounts and merely nodded at her whenever she saw them.

It seemed so pointless, being here in London all by herself without her father. He'd warned her that she wouldn't like it, and he was right. Most of the time she was cold and hungry – and, above all, lonely. Her English friend, Margot, was busy with war work, and besides she lived on the other side of the city. Her other best friend from school, Trudi, had stopped writing to her some time ago. Trudi's father was high up in the Nazi Party, and had told her that Kieran McCarthy was insulting the Führer with his lies. In her final letter, Trudi wrote that she was embarrassed that she and Catriona had ever been friends. The rejection hurt Catriona a lot, but there was nothing she could do about it.

Dust and plaster fell from the ceiling of the station as another huge bomb dropped overhead. The Central line was closest to her but it was the least deep of all the lines, so it felt the impact of the tonnes of incendiaries the most. She thought longingly of her bed. She had been taking a bath in the regulation five inches of water when the siren started. She had dragged on her nightie and dressing gown, pushing her feet into her shoes and run for the station. She tried to sleep, but the bench was hard and besides, she didn't want to keel over on the teenage boy sitting miserably beside her. The raid went on and on, hour after miserable hour as the people waited, until eventually the bombs grew fewer and fewer and then there was silence. The all-clear was sounded and wearily she dragged her aching body up the steps.

The city was burning. All around her, Londoners were emerging from shelters and tube stations to find their homes in flames, shops destroyed, roads decimated. Today seemed particularly bad. People milled about, picking their way through the rubble, some glassy-eyed and exhausted, others distraught as they searched for loved ones. Last May, Prime Minister Chamberlain had stood aside and been replaced by Winston Churchill and now Churchill's promise of blood, toil, tears and sweat was certainly being realised.

Catriona trudged home past the smoking bomb sites. She wondered if this raid would be on the front page of the Daily Express today. The reporters wrote endless copy on the brutish behaviour of Hitler and his Nazis, but they were scant in the detail of London bombings, passing it off as much less catastrophic than it actually was. Morale was bad enough and anyway, they didn't want Hitler to think they'd been cowed.

As Catriona made her way back to her own street, flames, smoke, the smell of smouldering materials filled the air. A water hydrant had been hit and some ARP wardens were trying to fix it as she skirted around the spray. At least their house was still standing. The terraced redbrick had its windows taped and the downstairs window had cracked but remained in place. She'd try to patch it up with more tape after work.

She let herself in and turned on the gas heater to take the sting of cold out of the air. The tea caddy stood beside the empty bread bin and she groaned when she discovered there was less than a teaspoon of tea left. The rations were never enough, even when Kieran was away and she had double. She spooned the precious leaves into a cup and put the kettle on the gas ring, which miraculously still worked.

While waiting for it to boil, she went upstairs to dress for work, trying to ignore her lovely warm bed. She would give anything to crawl under the covers and sleep but that kind of behaviour didn't win the war. As she peeled off her filthy dressing gown and nightie, black with smuts and fumes, the hem soaked because she couldn't avoid the puddles, she heard a knock on the door downstairs. Probably one of the neighbours checking up on her. They knew she was alone, and they were very kind. Something about war made people more considerate for each other, she'd found.

She popped her head out of the upstairs window but she didn't recognise the man in the hat and coat below. 'Hello?' she called down.

He looked up and took a step back to see her better.

'Catriona McCarthy?' He appeared to be in his fifties, short and heavy and he had a French regional accent which sounded familiar but which she couldn't quite place.

'Yes, look, hang on a tick, I'll come down.' She pulled a dress over her head, slipped her feet back into shoes, and went down to open the door, stepping outside rather than inviting him in. She didn't want to be rude, but something about this stranger made her uneasy. She held the front door half-shut behind her.

'I'm Catriona McCarthy, can I help you?'

'May I come in? I have a question for you.' His eyes showed no expression and her feeling of unease grew stronger.

'I'd rather you just asked me here, in the street.'

He hesitated, and then said, in his accented English, 'I wish to know, do you know where your father is?'

Catriona nearly ran back into the house and slammed the door. She knew her father had enemies all over Europe – but here, in London? Maybe one of Hitler's henchmen had tracked him down...

As if sensing she was about to flee, the man caught her wrist and whispered, *'Mademoiselle, c'est très important, il faut que je vous parlez. Je suis un ami personnel de Gaston.'*

Catriona stifled her panic. Now he'd told her where he was from, she realised it was true: he definitely had the accent of Saint-Émilion. But why would her mother's brother Gaston, of all people, send a strange man to enquire about her father? Due to her grandparents' distaste for their daughter's husband, the two men had barely met.

'Comment connaissez-vous mon oncle?' she asked, suspiciously. How do you know my uncle?

. . .

He glanced surreptitiously around, still holding her arm. *'Nous travaillons ensemble.'*

That wasn't good enough. Gaston was the vineyard owner now, since Mémé and Pépé had retired to a *manoir* on the estate. He was the boss. People worked *for* him, not *with* him. Still though, something stopped her from screaming out loud for help.

'What is his son called?' she asked quickly, in English, shaking off the man's hand.

He answered promptly, 'Loic.'

'And which is his best vintage?'

The man smiled. 'The '37 of course. He keeps twelve full cases in the back of the deep cellar behind the water tank under the lilac tree. My family have a vineyard in the same Department as yours, though I am a professor of Greek at the University of Bordeaux. You do not need to be afraid of me, Mademoiselle Catriona. I do not plan to harm you or your father. I wish merely to ask …'

'Which vineyard is your family's?' she interrupted. She wasn't going to give away anything, not until she was sure.

'Chateau de Riseau. It has a black railing all around and an ornamental pond in the front with... how do you say it… *le martin pêcheur...*'

'A kingfisher!' she cried, in amazement.

'Yes, yes, a kingfisher. I recall you fell in that pond when you were a child.'

She was smiling now. 'My cousin Loic was chasing me and I tripped.' Still very surprised, but now sure this man was telling her the truth, she opened the door and allowed him to pass by her into the house. In the kitchen, the kettle was boiling and she switched off the ring: if anyone saw her wasting gas like that, she'd be in trouble. 'Would you like tea, Monsieur…?'

'Jean-Claude de Riseau.' He had removed his hat; he was

nondescript looking, with slightly thinning sandy hair and a prominent nose. She began to think there was something vaguely familiar about him. Even the name rang a distant bell.

'Tea, Monsieur de Riseau?' she asked again.

'Non, Mademoiselle.' Then he corrected himself: 'I am sorry, no thank you.'

'We can talk in French, if you prefer.'

'No, I must practise, I studied here, at Oxford and I graduated in 1925 but I forget much of what I learned. It will return but I must speak it. After all, ostensibly I am here to connect with an old colleague for a book I've been working on.'

'The Germans let you travel?'

'Nobody suspects an old teacher, and the German officer running our area is not the worst. Because we are in the unoccupied zone, I think allowing me to travel was a gesture at trying to convince us nothing has changed, but of course everything has been altered so drastically. Though that is not the real reason I am here… May I?' He gestured to a kitchen chair.

'Of course, but come into the sitting room, it's more comfortable.'

Leaving the tea, she led him into the large room at the front of the house and sat on the sofa while Jean-Claude took the fireside seat, perched on the edge of it with his hat in his hands, his brow furrowed.

'So Mademoiselle Catriona,' he said, 'I have been sent to you by your uncle Gaston to ask where is Kieran McCarthy.'

She shook her head, puzzled. 'Why does Gaston want to know my father's whereabouts? They've barely ever spoken to each other.'

'Let me explain. Some time ago, your father was badly beaten by the SS and barely escaped with his life…'

Catriona jerked upright in her seat, horrified. She remembered well her father's story about an angry husband. How stupid she'd been to believe him! 'He didn't tell me...'

He inclined his head. 'Of course not. He wouldn't have wanted you to worry. But that is what happened, and when he escaped, he made his way to the Chateau Saint-Émilion to hide while his wounds healed. Your uncle was happy to help your father for your sake, Catriona – even though hiding a wanted man from the Nazis was dangerous. The two of them talked a great deal about Hitler and the occupation and realised they were true brothers, not just reluctant brothers-in-law. Gaston was adamant that if the French only knew what was being done in their name, by Maréchal *Pétain* and the rest of the treacherous puppets we have to call our government, they would do more to resist the Nazis. And so Kieran decided to use his journalistic skills to...'

'To help the Resistance?' She felt her stomach churn in fear.

'Exactly. Only in September he was at Dakar in French West Africa where the Free French were trying, with the British, to attempt to land...'

Her heart missed a beat, 'No, you're wrong – he's been in America since the third week of September!'

He shook his head. 'No. He has been in Africa and France. The navy, under orders of the Vichy traitors, opened fire, and the expedition was called back. So your father wrote a pamphlet about the attempted landing, and the Vichy response of bombing Gibraltar, and I got it printed at the university, and we distributed it...'

'Oh!' The danger took Catriona's breath away, and her stomach churned in fear for Kieran.

Jean-Claude nodded gravely. 'And he had other projects planned. A few weeks ago, he heard Hitler was meeting Pétain in Montoire to make sure Vichy was in line with the

Nazi regime. Your father had seen what that meant in real terms in Germany and he was determined to let the French know the reality of what they faced if they didn't resist. But now nobody has seen him or heard from him in over a fortnight. And if he hasn't turned up here in London…' He stopped, staring down at the carpet.

Catriona stood up, her heart hammering. 'Please tell me what you mean, Monsieur.'

'I mean, we fear he's been… betrayed.'

Catriona heard the words, but it was as if they had come from far away – underwater almost. Her father was all she had. Kieran had talked of the fate of those who went against the Nazis and were caught, yet somehow she never believed he would come to any harm. He was a daredevil, he took chances, his stories were often hair-raising and hilarious in equal measure, but he always got out. She said wildly, 'So at least he's not dead? He's still alive, in prison – or they might have let him go and he's disappeared to stay safe?'

Pity and sadness warmed his brown eyes. 'Catriona, I do not want to give you false hope.'

She collapsed on the sofa, and Jean-Claude came and sat beside her. He put his arm around her and she allowed her head to lie on his shoulder, but no tears came. She was frozen.

After what seemed like a long time, she felt strong enough to stand up. 'Thank you, Jean-Claude, for coming over to tell me. It means a lot. That was a hard job.' She could barely get the words out of her mouth. She wanted to be alone and he seemed to sense that. He stood up and gently placed both hands on her shoulders, kissing her on both cheeks.

'Merci, Mademoiselle Catriona. You may have an Irish accent and an Irish passport but, *vous etes une française fidèle.* I wish I could take you home, to be with your family. But France, I am sad to say, is no place for anyone now. Here,

Hitler's bombs rain down, but you live as free people. Cherish it and repel them when they come.'

He saw himself out.

After he left, she crossed the room to the fireplace. On the mantelpiece was the photo of her and her father, taken on a day trip to Brighton. She picked it up and looked at his handsome, smiling face.

'Don't leave me, Kieran, I need you,' she whispered, and only then did she allow her tears to fall.

CHAPTER 4

December, 1940. London

SHE WALKED QUICKLY along Horse Guards Avenue, in the direction of Whitehall.

It felt strange to be back among people again. For days after Jean-Claude had left her she'd stayed at home, sleeping or sitting for hours staring into space. She hadn't even contacted her work to say she wouldn't be in. No-one from the Daily Express had contacted her either. Probably they assumed she'd been killed or injured in an air raid. She wasn't even sure she wanted to go back to work. There was still a little money in her father's bank account, to which she had access. She contemplated using it to return to Dublin, and perhaps make contact with her father's family. But his parents had never shown any interest in their half-French granddaughter and she barely knew them – so how could she just walk into their life?

From time to time, she tried to face the fact that Kieran

might be dead. She even made an effort to picture her parents together in heaven – as the nuns had taught her to believe – but she couldn't. She had no sense of them, no feelings that they were near her. If they'd both left her, she was totally alone in the world.

This was why she was going to Whitehall, to the war office. She needed someone to tell her what to do, and how to go about finding a missing person in France. Undoubtedly they would look at her like she was mad, but she had to try. If her father was alive, and she had to believe he was – despite what Jean-Claude might think – she needed to do something to help him.

The government building took up almost the entire street, with two ornate turret-style structures on either end. She pushed through the enormous door and went inside. The foyer was busy with lots of people, many in uniform, milling around. She made her way through the crowd. Cream and black marble pillars stood to her left and right, and black and white chequered tiles covered the floor. At the back of the imposing foyer was a massive marble staircase. A girl around her own age was descending the steps. Catriona waylaid her at the foot of the stairs.

'Excuse me…'

The girl paused and looked enquiringly at her.

'I need to speak to someone…'

'Who?' snapped the girl, her brow furrowed. All around them were people walking very fast – everyone here seemed to be rushing somewhere.

'I... I'm not sure. I want to ask about...' She stumbled over her words. What did she want to ask about? 'A missing person, how to find them.'

The girl sighed. 'With the bombing and everything people are all over the place, so I have no idea – but look, I must get on. Perhaps you should try the police?'

Catriona stood feeling like a fool as the girl clipped away on high heels across the tiles. Then she turned and left the building, her cheeks burning. This was stupid, she thought, as she walked despondently up Whitehall in the direction of Trafalgar Square. Everywhere were piles of rubble and abandoned bits of furniture. It was coming up to Christmas but it didn't feel like it. There were hardly any decorations and the rationing meant there was little chance of anything but a meagre feast on Christmas Day. Margot had invited her to spend Christmas with her family but she had declined. She had told nobody that Kieran was missing and she couldn't face the questions from Margot's well-meaning parents.

She wracked her brain. Who else could she ask about her father? She had already contacted Reuters, but since Kieran McCarthy was a freelance, they only had dealings with him when he was submitting copy and had no way of knowing anything else about him. It was as if he'd never existed.

Passing the fogged-up windows of a Lyons Corner House, she realised she was hungry. It had been two weeks since Jean-Claude's visit and she'd barely eaten. She pushed the door open and immediately was greeted by a friendly waitress. The smell of cooking and the hubbub of chatter was strangely comforting. The Londoners sitting at the tables were clearly shattered and many were injured, but they no longer looked as traumatised as they had at the start of the Blitz. There was a growing resilience to these people that she found fascinating.

Kieran had told her it was the same in Ireland when her country had been occupied by the British, and terrorised by the Black and Tans and the Auxiliary forces up until 1921. There was defiance and a toughness there. Perhaps it was the way with all humans when faced with serious adversity? She didn't know; she certainly didn't seem to feel it herself.

She took a seat at one of the few empty tables and

ordered tea and toast. The food and her drink arrived and she took a bite but suddenly her hunger was gone. A familiar wave of despair passed over her. She fought the panic. She could not fall apart, she needed to go on. She caught the eye of a harassed-looking woman in her thirties who was trying to feed two children some very fatty-looking bacon and greasy egg, cut up and mashed together with watery tinned tomatoes.

'Please Olivier, you'll get very sick if you don't eat.' The woman was clearly exasperated but the little boy of about five stubbornly refused to open his mouth. Then the woman tried the other, slightly older child. 'Why don't you at least taste it, Valerie? It's nice!'

'C'est degoûtant,' said the little girl, wrinkling her nose to show her disgust.

'Well, I don't know what that means but please, *merci*, oh blast it anyway, that's the other one – *See Vou Play?'* she tried, but both children shook their heads obstinately.

Intrigued, Catriona called over, 'Can I help? I speak French.'

The woman smiled at her gratefully. 'Please do. They were found outside Paris but we don't even know who they are or who their parents are. My father-in-law was there on business when the Nazis invaded, and he came on these two lost in the chaos, they sort of latched onto him and he felt he had no option but bring them back here. My husband is away in the navy and we don't have any children of our own, so I'm trying to take care of them. But it's a disaster. I can't speak to them, they won't eat properly for me, they refuse to learn English, I'm at my wit's end.'

Catriona turned her smile to the two children. *'Je m'appelle Catriona et ma Maman est française. Comment vous appelez-vous?'*

The little girl turned her dark eyes to Catriona's face and

stared intently at her, sizing her up. Her brother alternated his glance between his sister and Catriona, gauging everything. Neither child spoke.

Catriona fought the urge to go on, and simply waited.

Eventually the girl spoke. *'Je m'appelle Valérie et mon frère s'appelle Olivier. J'ai huit ans et il a cinq ans. Savez-vous où sont notre Maman et Papa?'*

Catriona melted to see the bewilderment and loss in the little girl's eyes. Something in her saw herself reflected there. Olivier moved closer to his sister and she held his hand.

Honesty was always the best option.

'No,' she replied in French. 'It's nice to meet you Valérie and Olivier. You are being very brave children considering you are only eight and five years old. Now, I don't know where your parents are, I wish I did, but until we can find them, this nice lady is trying her best to look after you and she's worried because you won't eat properly.'

'Nous détestons tout,' Valérie said with a pout.

Catriona turned to the anxious woman. 'They are asking me if I know where their parents are and saying that they don't like any of the food. I could cook them something French, if you like. I don't have anything else to do today. Would that help?'

The woman looked pleasantly surprised at such a suggestion. 'Would you really? That really is too kind, and in any other circumstances, I would say not to dream of putting yourself out like that, but they barely eat and I'm getting more and more worried about them. They cry at night and I can't comfort them...' Her eyes filled with tears. 'I've contacted the authorities several times but they just say if it is at all possible for me to keep them, then I should. Everything seems so chaotic… I'm sorry, I didn't even introduce myself, my name is Elsa Perkins.'

Catriona leaned over and shook her hand. 'Catriona, Catriona McCarthy. Nice to meet you.'

'That's an Irish accent if I'm not mistaken?'

'Yes, I'm Irish but my mother was French.'

'Well, if you can help me with these two then I will be eternally in your debt. I only live down the street. I don't know what I have at home that we could make something tasty with, but I suppose we can but try.'

Olivier allowed Catriona to hold his hand all the way to Elsa's small, terraced house. Valérie, however, remained aloof and stood watching suspiciously as Elsa searched her cupboards.

'I have some carrots and some potatoes and some ham I was going to make a stew with later? Do you think they would like a stew?'

Catriona stifled a smile. The British obsession with boiling every shred of flavour out of food appalled her but she was getting used to it. She crouched down to speak to the children. *'Voulez vous des crudités, des pommes frites et une tranche de jambon blanc?'*

They nodded excitedly. *'Oui Mademoiselle, s'il vous plait.'* She smiled at their enthusiasm at the suggestion of food they might recognise.

She explained to Elsa that she was going to parboil the potatoes and then chop them into strips and fry them in a little oil, and then she was going to chop the carrots and serve them raw and accompany the vegetables with a slice of cold ham.

'Would they not rather have it all cooked together?' Elsa asked, amazed.

'No, definitely not,' Catriona said firmly. 'They are more used to it this way.'

The children soon polished off the simple but much more palatable meal, much to Elsa's relieved astonishment. They were just dipping cubes of bread in oil and vinegar when there was a knock on the door, which Elsa rushed to open.

Catriona looked up from clearing the dishes to see a tall grey-haired man enter the small kitchen with her new friend. He had a livid scar running from his temple to inside his shirt collar and walked with a distinct limp – as many of his generation did, due to injuries sustained in the last war.

'Catriona, this is my father-in-law Colonel Justin Perkins. Justin, this is the lifesaver Catriona McCarthy. I met her in a café today and she speaks French so she's chatting to the children and has made them some food they were actually happy to eat.'

'Hello, Colonel Perkins,' said Catriona, drying her hands on the tea towel.

He shook her hand gravely. 'Justin please, and may I call you Catriona?'

'Of course.' She was a little taken aback at his informality. He seemed to be very proper in his dress and demeanour but perhaps she had him wrong.

'Would you like a cup of tea?' Elsa offered.

'Yes my dear, that would be lovely,' he replied, patting Olivier on the head and smiling warmly at Valérie.

The children seemed to melt a little more now that their rescuer was here. He extracted a small paper bag from his pocket and produced two small lollipops, which made them smile – the first time Catriona had seen either of them smile since she met them. She wondered how he managed to get them; sweets were very hard to come by. They took their treats and left the table to go out into the little garden where there was a football and a very old-looking toy tea set.

Watching them, the old man said, 'These pair of imps somehow ended up in my care in the chaos that was the exodus out of Paris. I only have schoolboy French and I had no idea what they were saying to me. I had no real plan to bring them home with me but they seemed to sort of cling to me, goodness knows why, and nobody else was interested in looking after the little mites. When I got to the coast I couldn't leave them, they'd sort of followed me, so I took them with me. I didn't think any further than getting them here to be honest. Have you managed to ascertain anything about who they are?'

Catriona had chatted with them as she prepared dinner, and they'd told her how they had to run out of their home without even bringing the cat. Their father drove for a while but then the roads were full and they had to stop and get out of the car. There was lots of loud bangs, like enormous balloons being popped. Valérie saw her parents fall to the ground and then someone dragged her and Olivier into a big building full of hay and when everything went quiet again they couldn't find their Maman and Papa. There were so many people lying down on the road and none of them would get up. Other people were rushing around screaming. The children wandered up and down crying for someone to help them but nobody did, until Justin found them.

'Their names are Valérie and Olivier Moreau. Their father works in an office, their parents are called Jean-Luc and Evangeline and they live in the sixth arrondissement.'

'Well, not anymore they don't,' he sighed. 'I suppose their parents were killed.' He changed the subject. 'And you speak French because of your mother?'

'And because I was educated in Belgium, the German speaking part.'

'In Belgium. Fascinating. You speak German too, I suppose?' he asked, stirring his tea.

'Yes,' she admitted. 'Though I probably shouldn't say that out loud these days.'

'And what,' Justin asked, 'is a trilingual Irish girl doing wandering around poor battered London, might I ask?'

Catriona felt a lump in her throat. Apart from Margot, who was now off training for the WAAFs, she had no real friends in London and Elsa and Justin seemed so kind. To her horror, tears began to course hotly down her cheeks. She wiped them in frustration.

'Oh Catriona, what's wrong?' asked Elsa, placing her hand on hers.

The whole story came tumbling out and Elsa comforted her, as Justin watched with cool interest.

CHAPTER 5

March, 1941. London

Catriona stared at Justin as he stood facing her in her sitting room. He'd called very early, unannounced, as she was getting ready for work at the newspaper. What he was proposing was impossible.

'But I... I don't understand... I don't know anything about... anything. I don't think I'd be the right person at all.' She felt her heart pounding in her chest. The clock ticked on the mantelpiece, beside the framed photograph of herself with Kieran.

Justin nodded. 'I understand it's a shock. But the fact that you speak both French and German would be a tremendous advantage. I hate putting you in danger like this, but to be frank, I felt it would be remiss not to inform certain people about your existence. It's not my section actually, but when I heard your story I spoke to our people in that area…'

'What area?'

'Mm. That area where your French family live. And I'm afraid they agree with me that you are too good an opportunity to pass up.'

She had met Justin a number of times since December, all at Elsa's house – including on Christmas Day when he'd turned up with sweets and little wooden toys for the children. He'd always seemed very interested in Catriona's life, but she'd thought he was just being polite.

Today was a revelation.

Justin was not, it seemed, a business man, but someone working for the British government who had found out a lot about her father. He was vague on the details. 'They believe he was on the brink of something, something really big that could turn things around... Before, that is, he fell off the surface of the earth, so to speak.'

Catriona stared at him. Slowly the extraordinary reality was sinking in. First Jean-Claude had told her that Kieran was working on behalf of the Resistance, spreading true information about the Nazi occupation. Now Justin was telling her that her father had also been spying on behalf of the British. She said weakly, 'I had no idea about my father's life.'

He patted her arm. 'I'm sure it was to protect you my dear, not that he didn't trust you. I have come to know you a little in recent weeks and I find you to be a most trustworthy young woman. A worthy successor to your father.'

'A... *what?*'

'Indeed. The work he was doing was very important, very important indeed. They need someone to carry it on, and have come to the conclusion that you are the best person for the job. If you agree to do this, Catriona, you must understand, they are not sending you to find Kieran McCarthy, they are sending you to continue his mission. Do you understand? If you find your father alive, that is a bonus for you – but it is not the purpose of your journey.'

In a state of shock, Catriona heard herself saying, 'And what would I have to do?'

Justin opened the brown leather briefcase he carried with him everywhere. He extracted a photograph and handed it to her. 'That,' he explained, 'is Frederik Schroeder. He's a German officer stationed near Saint-Émilion.'

She stared at the picture. A pleasant-looking young man with short blonde hair gazed back at her. He was laughing, his eyes crinkled up with merriment. She judged him to be around thirty. She looked up at Justin in puzzlement.

His kindly gaze held hers. 'Catriona, what I am about to tell you cannot ever be discussed with anyone else. It is of the utmost importance that this information remains in strictest confidence. Do you understand?'

Catriona swallowed. 'Yes.' Her voice was barely audible.

'Good. Listen carefully. Oberleutnant Schroeder's mother is French, like yours. His father is German, and served in the last war. Frederik graduated in law at the University of Heidelberg in 1935. He is, according to your father, appalled by the brutal and illegal nature of the occupation. Making the French pay for their own occupation, for example, it is nothing short of organised plunder and is leading to mass malnutrition. Schroeder is particularly horrified by the way local men and women are being shipped off to work in Germany under this so-called *Service du Travail Obligatoire*.'

'How good of him,' murmured Catriona.

He raised his eyebrows. 'Not all Germans are outright psychopaths, you know.'

'Perhaps not. But this Schroeder is a Nazi officer, isn't he?'

'True. Yet your father felt he could recruit him to our side.'

'What?'

'And now your father is... has disappeared, we need someone else to go to this young man, to earn his trust and finish the job. To recruit someone of his rank to our side – well, it could be very significant.'

She could hardly believe what she was hearing. 'You want me to recruit Schroeder? How?'

The tall grey-haired man paced up and down the narrow room. 'Get close to him. We feel that the fact that you speak both French and German would allow a level of intimacy that we could not achieve with someone else. Schroeder must be seen to be hard on the locals in order to maintain his trusted position with his superior officers, but a dalliance with a pretty girl is allowed...'

'A dalliance?' Catriona was genuinely shaken. The British wanted her to form an actual relationship with a Nazi officer?

Justin either didn't notice, or else ignored, her shocked expression. 'Your uncle will be useful in arranging an introduction. Schroeder is a regular visitor to your family's vineyard. He knows nothing of Gaston's true politics, nor – fortunately for all concerned – of Gaston's relationship with your father.' Justin picked up the photo of Catriona and Kieran from the mantelpiece. 'Even better, you look nothing like your father, so Schroeder will never make the connection. We don't *think* he had anything to do with your father's disappearance but...'

Ice cubes jostled in the pit of her stomach. 'But you think he might?'

He set the photo back down. 'One can never be entirely sure about anything in this war. Nonetheless, we trust your father's judgement and think Schroeder is worth pursuing.'

'Because he could...?'

'Because, Catriona, as your father understood, Bordeaux

is the main centre of Nazi power in that area and it is France's largest port and therefore of huge significance for both us and the enemy. Who controls it will be vital, and if we had inside knowledge of the Nazi war machine…' He turned to face her, with a serious gaze. 'Well then, it would be a huge boost for us. You would be doing this country a great service, and your own as well…'

'Ireland is neutral.'

'Of course. But you're half-French? Still, it must be your choice. And I'm sure I needn't tell you that the consequences will be dire if you are caught. Torture, deportation, death… The Nazis stop at nothing, not even when it comes to a pretty girl.'

Catriona sank down slowly onto the sofa, allowing these last words to hang in the air between them.

What would her father say about all this? Surely he would refuse point blank to consider allowing his daughter to be put in such danger. But her father wasn't here. And if this Schroeder had been a genuine friend to him, and perhaps knew where he was...

If you are caught, the consequences will be dire.

Justin stood with his hands behind his back, peacefully staring into the empty fireplace, leaving her to make her choice.

Torture, deportation, death... The Nazis stop at nothing, not even when it comes to a pretty girl.

But then Catriona thought of her mother's family in Saint-Émilion suffering under Nazi rule. And of the Belgian nuns who'd educated her, and London in flames, and then of Valérie and Olivier, praying every night for '*Maman et Papa*' to come and find them.

'When would I have to go?' Her voice sounded stronger than she felt.

'We can get you out on the next full moon. The last one is

just gone, so three to four weeks' time.' Justin didn't seem remotely surprised by her answer. 'You'll need to be briefed, prepared and your cover story made water tight. The Germans are very sensitive to new people in any area, so we will make sure to give you a good back story. Your accent will be analysed by our people and an appropriate profile invented for you.'

He took a card out of his pocket and handed it to her. It was an address on Baker Street. 'Just present yourself at that address tomorrow morning at nine. They'll be expecting you. Tell nobody what you are doing or where you are going.'

'I would like to say goodbye to Elsa and the children.' Since before Christmas, she'd been going there after work every day to help Elsa make French onion soup, potatoes dauphinoise, cheese omelettes, crepes and a few other cheap and simple French dishes. She'd also begun teaching the children to speak and read English, and even did a little arithmetic with them.

He looked sympathetic. 'That's not possible, I'm afraid. Perhaps write them a letter, saying you had to go back to Ireland in a hurry. Family crisis of some sort. Does that sound all right?'

He offered her his outstretched hand and, speechless, she shook it then held on to it for a moment. She didn't ever want to let it go. He was the last link to safety, to her normal life.

'I do hope we'll see each other again, Catriona,' he said, as he gently withdrew his fingers. 'The best of luck, my dear.'

CHAPTER 6

May, 1941. Chateau de Clairand, Saint-Émilion, France

CATRIONA KNEW that she looked French in every imaginable way. Every stitch of her clothing was French, and no detail was left to chance. Even the way French women buttoned their blouses was different – but she knew that anyway. Luckily she looked more like her French mother than her Irish father so it was unnecessary to do too much to her appearance. The rationing in London had melted away any slight curves she might have had and she was as thin as all the other women she saw daily.

For twenty-six days in London, she had stayed at the Baker Street house – never once venturing outside. She was schooled on how French women wore make-up, drilled on what was and wasn't in the shops so she wouldn't blow her cover by asking for something that had not been available for months. Every aspect of life under German occupation had been taught to her over and over, day and night, to ensure her safety. The woman who ran the Baker Street house was kind but took no nonsense. She'd explained how most agents had months of training, and how Catriona was in grave danger if she slipped up in any way.

The days passed in a blur. She was given a new name, Emilie Barrau, and as each day passed Catriona McCarthy seemed further and further away. She neither spoke nor heard any English. In French and German, she learned each rank of German soldier based on his insignia, and she was interrogated on her cover story relentlessly.

One night, she was pulled from her narrow bed in one of the attic rooms and brought roughly downstairs. Sitting at the battered desk in the front office were two men she'd never seen before, wearing civilian clothes. They interrogated her, switching seamlessly from French to German to English, constantly trying to trip her up. Despite feeling disorientated, she maintained her story, answering when they spoke in French or German but never when they spoke in English.

'Wer sind deine Eltern?' one of the men barked in German, demanding to know who her parents were.

'Henri *und* Camille Barrau,' she responded in German.

'Dates of birth?' another asked, in English this time.

'Je ne comprends pas l'anglais...'

'Date de naissance de vos parents?' His accent was bad, definitely not a native speaker.

'My father was born on the third of January 1899, and my mother on the twelfth of March 1901,' she replied in flawless French.

The French man who interviewed her on one of the first days she was at Baker Street, told her handlers that her accent wasn't entirely pure but the story that she was from the French-speaking part of Belgium should cover it. The danger wasn't the Germans, because such subtlety of accent was beyond even those who were fluent in French; the danger was with French collaborators. The French were very sensitive to even the slightest discrepancy in accent, so her back story would have to reflect that.

'Where?' the first man asked, again in English – but this time quietly, almost bored.

Catriona shrugged, in that Gallic way she'd always done.

'Où?' he asked in French.

'My father is from Lyon, Rue Sainte Justine, my mother is from a small village in Belgium – Pont Veille, in the Ardennes.'

One of the men came up behind her and spoke quietly into her ear, 'And why are you in Bordeaux?' in English.

She didn't reply. He repeated the question in German.

Catriona trotted out her story, word perfect – she was here to work – but jumped as the other man brought his fist down on the table forcefully and shouted at her. *'Lügnerin!* Liar!' She tried not to look terrified.

'We know you are not who you say you are!' Spittle from his lips landed on her cheek and she could smell his sour breath. She felt tears prick the back of her eyes.

'Je ne comprends pas...' she began again, a teardrop escaping.

The man grabbed her face and squeezed her jaw, forcing her head to turn painfully. He repeated the statement in German this time.

For the next hour they shouted questions at her in all three languages, in rapid-fire succession, and though she felt flustered and confused she didn't make a mistake. Eventually they let her go back to bed. She had passed the test.

The remainder of the days went by in a blur. Every single

item of her own was taken and stored. She was given a whole new identity, a new wardrobe, a French hairdo. One frightening day, she had a tooth hollowed out and a lethal cyanide pill inserted. It was covered in a rubber casing to prevent accidental death if swallowed inadvertently. The dentist explained that all she would need to do was dislodge the false tooth and bite down hard. The glass ampoule would crack and the poison would enter her bloodstream very quickly. Death, he assured her, would be instantaneous.

'Let's pray you never need to use it, but if they do capture you, then take it.'

The following day, she was told she was being flown over to France.

She was dropped by Lysander into a field south of Libourne on a moonlit night. There had not been enough time to train her to parachute so they mercifully allowed the plane to touch down for a second or two where she was dumped unceremoniously out, and before she knew what was happening, the Lysander was airborne again. She was met by a very gruff Frenchman who did not introduce himself. He was in his sixties, she guessed, with a bald head but very bushy eyebrows. He took her bag and pulled her into the shadows, his hand clamped on her forearm. He was strong and wiry and had a very pungent body odour, which made her gag. Without asking how she was or anything about her, he pulled two bicycles from a hedge. Shoving one at her, he fixed her small suitcase to the back of his. She would take to her grave the look of horror and disgust on his face when she told him that she didn't know how to ride a bicycle, because the nuns thought riding bicycles was unladylike.

'What? Are you serious?' he hissed the words at her in the corner of the dark field. 'What kind of a moron can't ride a bicycle? Listen Miss Ladylike,' he spat, 'there has been no petrol here for months now, so the only way to travel is on a bike. If you can't cycle and a German sees you he'll smell a rat instantly. He'll take you in, torture you and then kill you. Simple as that. So I'd suggest you pick it up pretty damned fast.'

'But how…'

'Just do it.' He exhaled in frustration and lit up a cigarette, nodding in the direction of the second bike.

Twenty minutes of furious, hissed instruction later, and four or five heavy falls, and she was wobbling along on her own. Under any other circumstances, she was sure it would have taken her much longer but her instructor was not a person to be trifled with.

They cycled over rough farmland until the morning sun began to streak across the sky. Despite the terrifying situation, Catriona felt strangely happy to be back in France. Before dawn gave way to morning he ushered her into an old barn, told her to go right down to the back and cover herself with hay.

'Someone will come for you later. In the meantime, sleep and be quiet.' And he was gone.

Catriona tried to ignore the scurrying of mice in the barn, or what she hoped were mice and not rats, and she did as she was told. She was bone tired, her legs aching, and she hadn't slept properly once she knew she was going to France, yet she didn't imagine sleep would come. She was too on edge.

* * *

'Catriona! Wake up! Wake up!'

She felt her shoulder being shaken and blearily she opened her eyes – then sat up with a gasp. 'Loic!'

She recognised her cousin crouching beside her instantly – the cousin who had once caused her to fall into the pool of

Jean-Claude's family chateau. Though she'd not seen him for three years, he was unforgettable with his dark curly hair and flashing dark eyes, almost black. Their grandmother used to call him her little gypsy. He looked nothing like his big brawny father and only a little like Marie-Clare, his mother. He was as lithe and tanned as when they were children, back in the days when he always out-ran or out-climbed her as they played in the huge trees around the chateau.

He was grinning at her. 'Yes it's Loic, and you are Emilie, and you look nothing like my cousin Catriona who was an annoying little girl and not a skinny sophisticated woman like yourself. Now come on, we must go, quickly.' He pulled her up.

The muscles in her legs ached and her buttocks were so numb they felt like they belonged to someone else. 'Please tell me we aren't going by bike,' she groaned and he chuckled.

'Maurice was not too happy with you, I can tell you. He works for us and is a great help but he is not known for his patience. But no, no bikes today. I have a pony and cart outside.'

'Oh thank God.' She brushed the straw from her dress and tried to rearrange her hair, while Loic scrutinised her from head to toe.

'You look far too glamorous for a job in a vineyard. Papa thought you might arrive dressed wrongly, so he gave me these for you.' He handed her a grey overall dress and a pair of flat shoes; a washed-out cotton headscarf completed the look. 'Change quickly, I'll turn around.'

Catriona did as she was told. The dress was horrible and smelled of stale sweat but she buttoned it up and tied the scarf around her head. As she dressed, he spoke again, barely above a whisper although they were alone in the barn:

'They are everywhere, the filthy Boche, and they are very

observant. They are particularly on the lookout for new faces, so if we run into anyone we'd better have our story straight. You're one of the workers for the *vendange*. We don't employ people in large numbers for the harvest until September but we do have about twenty casual people at the moment. None of them are local, so they won't recognise you from your holidays in the chateau. Make sure you stick to your story. You were born in French-speaking Belgium and educated in a convent in German-speaking Belgium. You moved to Paris to find work. In Paris you got talking to a guy called Armand. Armand's real, by the way, and don't worry about him – he's one of us. Anyway, Armand told you he was coming here for the *vendange* and gave you the address because the vineyard is always looking for new workers. Especially now, as so many of the local men and women have been sent to work camps.'

'Should I put these other clothes in my suitcase?'

'Yes – but don't show them to anyone. How do those fit?' He turned to look and burst out laughing. She pulled a silly face at him but then became business-like.

'Okay, I'm ready. Let's go.' This was not a game of dress up; she was here to do a job. Though how she was going to attract the attention of any man in this get up, let alone a high-ranking German officer, she was at a complete loss to discover.

The journey to the chateau was only nine kilometers, but once they had passed through the town of Libourne, Loic kept the cart to the back lanes, sometimes crossing through other vineyards rather than going on the main road, so that the journey took a full two hours. Out in open countryside they spoke quietly about their extended family and the new reality for France. But when they arrived at the chateau, Loic just dropped her off at the workers' quarters as he would have done with any other casual employee.

All day, Catriona worked – weeding, checking the leaves, nurturing the vines. The buds were breaking out now so it was important to train them along the correct lines and also to tie the clusters up between the wires. The Parisian, Armand, showed her how to thin the clusters, to remove the flowers. That night, as they went into the kitchen of one of the outbuildings where the staff were fed, he made a point of saying, 'So you made it out of Paris, eh? I'm glad you did, it was crazy back there.'

The other workers were all within earshot but they didn't seem to notice. They were too busy serving themselves their thin *cassoulet*, made up mostly of turnip, potatoes and bread made from chestnut flour from the large *bain-marie*, all washed down with water where once there would have been wine. The people in London had warned her that food shortages in France were even worse than England but nothing had prepared her for the hunger. All food producers, from the large farms to the cottage industries were forced to hand over much of their produce to the forces of occupation, leaving very little for themselves.

Taking her cue, Catriona replied, 'Yes and thank you for telling me about this place, I had nowhere to go otherwise.'

He shrugged. 'No problem. Any news of your family?'

She shook her head sadly. 'No, nothing. I've written and now that they have this address perhaps...'

Armand patted her on the shoulder. 'Please God it will work out for you.' He left her to join some of the older men at a long table. She sat with some women and girls her own age. She tried out her back story as they ate their meal and they accepted it without question. One woman from Lyon was curious about her accent so she explained about her Belgian upbringing and convent education, and her story was accepted and the conversation moved on.

Days passed in back-breaking and tedious work. She did

it without complaining but she was frustrated. There was no point to this: she'd come here to do a different job and she desperately wanted to get on with it. She hadn't seen this Schroeder, nor any other German for that matter, in the five days since she got here and had spoken to nobody about her mission.

At night – tossing and turning on her hard mattress – she hankered after her soft bed in the chateau nearby. Nor was it just her bed that she missed. She longed to see her grandparents, and her uncle and his wife, even though she knew they weren't allowed to acknowledge her as family.

The following evening, Loic approached her with an order. 'The boss wants the cellars cleaned in preparation for the new vintage. Be there with your cleaning equipment in half an hour.'

'Oui, Loic.' Delighted, Catriona collected a mop and bucket from the servants' quarters and made her way up to the magnificent chateau, whose image was represented on so many bottles of De Clairand Grand Cru. Crossing the lawn, she was surprised to see a familiar face – Jean-Claude de Riseau, the man who had come to her in London. He was deep in conversation with her uncle and neither man gave any hint of recognising her as she passed within a few yards of them.

The cellar door was open. She stepped inside and tiptoed cautiously down the dark, damp steps. Halfway down, she felt someone touch her arm. It was Loic, who had been waiting in one of the many alcoves. Wordlessly, he took the bucket from her and she followed him down a passageway off to the right. The cellar was ancient and smelled faintly of damp and earth and fermentation. It brought her instantly back to her childhood. The area under the chateau and the grounds was comprised of several tunnels that opened up into caves where the wine was stored. Some of the caves were locked behind a metal grill, and it was into one of these that Loic brought her. He pulled a cord on the ceiling and the small space was flooded in weak yellow light from a single bulb.

As her eyes adjusted, Catriona burst into sobs of happiness: her beloved grandparents were here to meet her! 'Mémé! Pépé!'

'Gaston arranged it…' Pépé embraced her, struggling to hold back his sobs. 'You've grown up, Catriona. You look so like our darling Eloise, it's as if she were standing in front of us…'

Tears were also running down Mémé's wrinkled face. She clung to Catriona. 'Ma p'tit chouette. Oh how we have longed to talk to you, it has been so hard, knowing you were here on the estate and not being allowed to see you – but Gaston insisted it was for your safety. Everywhere someone is watching, taking everything in. Oh Catriona, you're so thin, you need proper feeding.'

'Catriona, how wonderful to see you!' Gaston's gentle little wife, Marie-Clare, came running into the cellar and embraced her as well, kissing her lightly on both cheeks. Gaston and Jean-Claude followed.

'How nice to see you again, mademoiselle!' cried Jean-Claude, shaking her hand.

Gaston swept Catriona up in a warm, strong hug. 'I am sorry for ignoring you earlier, my dear, but any activity out of the ordinary is seen as suspicious and if anything were to happen to you…' Close up, her uncle looked older than she remembered, his large brow furrowed with care and his black hair more grey at the temples – but he was still her bear-like uncle Gaston. He used to carry her and Loic on his back and when she was a little girl she thought her uncle was the biggest man in the world. His wife Marie-Clare was tiny by comparison.

Hugging him back, she said, 'Thank you. Thank you so much for letting me see everyone. Just knowing you are all here, even if we can't acknowledge each other in public, gives me courage.'

Her grandmother burst into fresh tears. 'Please my darling, whatever you're doing here, be careful...'

Her husband put his arm around his wife. 'She is a brave girl and whatever she is doing, I am sure it's for the best.'

'But she is so young! Anything could happen to her!'

Catriona kissed her grandmother's wet cheeks. 'Mémé, I'll be fine. Now everyone, I need to talk to Gaston, alone.' She'd had it drilled into her from London: never discuss her mission with more than one person. The fewer people knew the details, the safer everyone would be.

Her grandmother protested at being banished so soon, but her grandfather kissed Catriona's forehead – just as he had always done since she was small – and murmured, *'Bon courage, ma chérie'* before leading his weeping wife away. Marie-Clare followed, with Loic and Jean-Claude.

As soon as she was alone with her uncle, she said in a low voice, 'I have instructions from London. I need you to introduce me to Oberleutnant Frederik Schroeder as soon as possible.'

Her uncle shuddered. 'I'm afraid for you, Catriona. I have to admit, I also think it's far too dangerous for you, a young girl...'

'Maybe so, but that is my mission. My father was on the point of recruiting Schroeder as an agent, before he disappeared. I've been sent here to complete the job.'

He frowned. 'Schroeder has a reputation as a man who turns a blind eye and bends the rules to spare the unfortunate. But you have to wonder... Is he as good as he seems? Your father believed in him, yet Oberleutnant Schroeder was probably one of the last men to see Kieran alive.'

'Oh…' The loud beating of her heart and a sudden wave of nausea made it hard for Catriona to answer right away. Finally, she whispered, 'So you think my father is definitely dead? And you think Schroeder may have had something to do with it?'

Gaston sighed and shook his head. 'We don't know. Nobody knows. Kieran has made no contact, though he had many ways of getting a message to me. The fact that I've not heard a whisper from him is not good, I have to be honest…'

It was hard for Catriona to restrain her grief, but she managed to say in a louder voice, 'Then that's all the more reason why I need you to help me get to meet this Schroeder. Maybe I can find the truth. I know it's not the purpose of the mission – I was told that a hundred times in London – but I need to know if my father is alive or dead. One way or the other.'

Gaston groaned. 'Very well. We will invite Schroeder for dinner. As far as the Germans are concerned, we de Clairands are – if not actual collaborators – at least not hostile. This suits us. We need to know what they are doing and the only way to do that is to be close to them. We often invite them here, fill them with wine – not the best you understand, but they are so uncultured they imagine it is – and listen carefully to their vulgar nonsense. You will be asked to serve at table. Wear your own clothes that you brought from London. Loic tells me they're very pretty. Then it's up to you. If he notices you, try to encourage him.'

'Encourage him how?' Suddenly her courage failed her, and she felt like a child again. She had spent her life in a convent and she knew nothing about men – if you didn't count creepy Mr Kingston. 'I don't even know what sort of woman he likes. What if he has a girl already? Or several?'

'I don't think he has. He doesn't seem to have anything to do with the local *collaborateurs horizontales.*'

Catriona winced at her uncle's description of those women who had sexual relations with the Germans, often for money. 'I don't want to be seen as one of them...'

Gaston looked aghast. 'I'm not suggesting... Look, Frederik Schroeder is an educated man. He often speaks of music – Beethoven and Mozart in particular. And he reads. So seducing him might be a more intellectual task than a physical one.'

'I'll try that then.' Her voice quavered.

Her uncle embraced her tightly, and kissed the top of her head. 'Ah, Catriona. You look so much like my little sister and she was brave like you. Nobody wanted her to marry your father – he wasn't the right stock shall we say – but she did it anyway. And he turned out to be a very fine man, and someone I was privileged to call a friend. I commend you, Catriona. Your mother would be so very proud of you, as am I. Now, go. If you are away from the other workers much longer, questions may be asked.'

He led her through the shadowy cellars to the steps that mounted to the lawn. When she was nearly at the door, he called to her from below. 'Do you see that weather vane near the lily pond?'

She could, through the open door – a small very old metal cockerel on a pole, only head height, throwing a long shadow across the grass in the lowering sun. It had been there for as long as she could remember.

'Yes?' she called softly, to where Gaston stood in the shadows.

'He's too rusty to move in the wind now. But if you need me, twist his head towards Jean-Claude's place, a quarter turn to the west, and then let yourself into the cellar. The spare key is...'

'In the knot hole under the lowest branch of the lilac tree,' she finished. She remembered Loic showing her, a lifetime ago when they were young.

'Good. Then come down here and wait for me. I'll get to you as soon as I can.'

She nodded and tried to remain composed. This was really happening. She stepped out into the pink sunset glow.

CHAPTER 7

August, 1941. Bordeaux

Wearing a cream silk robe, Catriona stood looking down out of the bay window at the Place de la Bourse. She was sipping a cup of rich dark Arabica, and eating a ripe peach. Real coffee beans, good food and fine clothes were but a distant memory for the French population trying to go about their business on the streets below, yet Catriona had everything she wanted. Frederik didn't live ostentatiously – unlike the other German officers, he refused to rob those sent to camps – but still his apartment was in the nicest part of the city, overlooking the elegant Pont de Pierre and the dome of Basilique Saint Michel.

Unsurprisingly, the locals resented Catriona's perceived good fortune. Just yesterday, a girl in a shop had been very rude to her when she and Frederik had been browsing, and Catriona was sure she'd heard the girl mutter '*collaborator horizontales'* under her breath when Frederik was out of earshot.

Catriona had performed well on the night of the dinner party, three months earlier. Frederik was the only guest, and she had managed to accidentally on purpose spill wine on his linen napkin, for which she apologised very sweetly in German. Later, when she was serving coffee on the balcony, Gaston and Marie-Clare managed to get 'called away' leaving Frederik and Catriona to chat for several minutes about the Beethoven symphony that Marie-Clare had left playing on the gramophone in the background. Catriona had had to dredge up all she learned from Soeur Rosarie, her old music teacher, to keep up with Frederik's knowledge of the composer, but he still seemed to find her fascinating.

That night, as she helped Frederik into his coat, she caught Gaston's eye and saw the pain there. She could imagine how he felt, seeing her in danger like this. But maybe nothing would come of it…

The following day Frederik called around and asked to take her out. She feigned reluctance at first.

'Look,' he said. 'I know it's not good for nice French girls like you to be seen with us, but I promise we can be very discreet. I'm not like the others, I swear to you. I just want to talk, I haven't had a real conversation since I got here, and I miss it. Please Emilie, we can do whatever you want.'

Finally, she had agreed to meet him two days later.

She had no experience with men, and could never picture herself as the Femme Fatale type, but neither she nor Frederik were very experienced. He told her he'd had a few girlfriends at university but nothing serious, and certainly nothing like this. He said the women who went with his fellow officers, with their elaborate hair and makeup, and their flirtatious ways, kind of intimidated him.

After only three weeks, Frederik told her he was being

transferred to Bordeaux and suggested she leave her work and move in with him. She was almost paralysed with terror, yet somehow she steeled herself to say yes. And here in Bordeaux, she had begun to feel oddly safe around him. He was funny and interesting and so kind to her. The only time he scared her was when he spoke mockingly about his colleagues behind their backs. She feared then that he was laying a trap for her, and took care never to mock them herself. Instead, she treated his colleagues with great respect. When they came round to for dinner, she cooked, served cocktails and offered them cigarettes.

Two officers in particular were regular visitors: Otto Schmidt was sanctimonious and full of himself; Karl Fischer was lecherous and a dedicated Nazi. They drank a lot, and were careless in their talk, and when they were, she listened carefully. It surprised her that they were so indiscreet around her – maybe it was because Frederik so obviously trusted his Belgian mistress. Not only did he let her sit in on their after-dinner conversations, he had also given her a rather expensive camera for her (pretended) birthday, with which she took pictures of them all.

One photo of the three of them, smiling with raised glasses on the balcony, captured the moment when Karl had just announced the latest decree from Berlin, which was that anyone suspected of helping the Resistance in any way at all should be shot on sight.

This decree – and everything else of importance, including the film from the camera – she passed on to Fabien, who worked as a waiter in the café on the corner of the Rue Ste Catherine.

A message came back to her from Gaston, via Fabien, telling her she was doing wonderfully and that she was right to make Frederik trust her before attempting to draw him in. The photographs she had taken, not just of German officers but also of documents she came across around the apartment were of particular use to the Résistance. She made sure to have separate rolls, ones she gave to Frederik to have developed, no such luxury was available to ordinary French people anymore, and the ones she passed on to Gaston. Oddly, the praise made her feel a twinge of guilt for deceiving the Oberleutnant. On the one hand, he might be the man who had betrayed her father, but on the other…well, that was irrelevant, he was now her lover and she had a job to do.

They had so much in common it almost troubled her. He too had a French mother, and had spent his childhood summers in France. He complimented her on her German, though he smiled at some of her Belgian phrases. A week ago – after too much wine – he had told her how lonely he was, how he hated this war and how much of an imposter he felt when his father told everyone that his son was a good German. 'I don't feel like a good German,' he confessed.

They were sitting on the balcony, the lights of Bordeaux glittering beneath them. She turned her empty glass in her hand, heart fluttering. 'But you are German.'

'I am. And I love the Germany of my childhood. But it is Hitler's Germany now…'

'You're an officer in Hitler's army.'

He shrugged. The wine loosening his tongue, perhaps. 'I follow my orders, but not zealously. I am guilty of turning a blind eye to goods being traded on the black market, or Jewish children being passed off as true French…'

'But you do support Hitler?'

He hesitated. 'Look. I understand why he is popular. The Treaty of Versailles brought Germany to its knees, and then Hitler arrives and says we won't put up with it anymore, we won't be dictated to by the English or French or Americans, and you can see why people worship him for that. But the reality of what he is doing in Germany and in every country that he invades… The deportations… I feel…'. He stopped and refilled her glass, then said hotly: 'Just last week they opened a huge internment camp in Drancy outside Paris. More will be rounded up, sent there, or worse. Pétain has established military courts on his own people. My mother must be turning in her…' But then he stopped and shrugged carelessly, and said, 'I'm boring you with politics, darling. Let's talk about music, and gaze at the stars.' And he raised his glass to the night sky that glittered above them.

At that moment, she wondered if she should tell him who she was and ask him what he knew about her father. She was sure Frederik loved her, and that he was by no means a committed Nazi. Yet still some fearful instinct told her no, and Kieran had always warned her to trust her gut. Frederik Schroeder had been promoted from *Saint-Émilion* to Bordeaux, so someone high up in the Nazi Party clearly trusted him to do his job. So perhaps the Oberleutnant was only pretending to appear sympathetic to the French; perhaps he was trying to trick her into revealing herself? It was so hard to know how to move forward.

In the meantime, what she was doing was far from useless – she was passing on valuable information and members of the Resistance were being forewarned and lives saved by her actions. Maybe she should keep on doing just that and hope that Frederik let something slip about Kieran by accident.

And then, two days ago, as they were going for a drive in the countryside, she had seen the sign for Chateau Kirwan with its welcome written in the Irish language.

'*Céad Míle Fáilte* – "a hundred thousand welcomes"!' she exclaimed in surprise, pointing at the inscription under the family name before she realised what she'd done.

'How do you know that?' he asked, glancing sidelong at her, bemused.

'Oh…' She thought quickly. 'There was an Irish girl in my class at boarding school and she taught me a little of her language and history. Did you know France tried to liberate the Irish from the English in 1798? They landed in Mayo, but got defeated…' She stopped speaking suddenly, worried he would make some cynical joke about the French army having been recently defeated by the Germans.

Instead, he merely nodded. 'Interesting. I'd like to go to Ireland someday. I've been told that it's beautiful. Or at least according to this Irish fellow I knew...' His voice trailed off suddenly.

Catriona sat staring straight ahead, gripping her knees. Her heart pounded; it was hard to breathe normally. 'Irishman?' She mustn't sound too interested.

He was smiling as he drove. 'Yes. Nice chap.'

'I'd love to meet him. Is he still around?'

'Not anymore.'

'What happened to him?'

Luckily, he was too busy taking a corner to notice the shake in her voice. 'Went back to Ireland, I assume. The last I heard of him, he was boarding a train for Paris. Karl mentioned seeing him at the station.'

Her heart throbbed with hope. 'And Karl was sure it was him?'

This time, he glanced oddly at her. 'What has you so interested in my Irishman?'

She turned her head away to hide the shine in her eyes. 'I don't know. I got the feeling you liked him.'

'Mm. That's true. Maybe I'll chase him up, after the war. *Donnerwetter!'* A cat dashed in front of the car, causing Frederik to swerve. Later, she tried to return to the subject but he no longer wanted to talk about it – the moment was gone.

Now, two days later, she was standing at the bay window, sipping coffee and still trying to work out if Kieran

McCarthy had really got on a train and gone to Paris before he disappeared. Or if her Nazi lover was telling her outright lies.

The next moment, Frederik's strong arms circled her waist and his warm lips kissed her neck. *'Mein liebling!* Come back to bed, it's still early.'

She said absently, her mind still on her father, 'No, I'm wide awake now.'

'Exactly. Come back to bed with me for an hour. We might not have that much longer together, if I'm sent to the Russian front.'

'To Russia?' She stiffened in his arms, shocked. 'Is that likely?'

He seemed gratified to have troubled her; he turned her to face him and ran his hand through her silk blonde hair. 'Have I upset you? I'm glad.'

'Of course I'm upset.' Her voice was shaking and she realised, to her dismay that she actually meant what she'd said – she *was* upset. Did she have real feelings for him? No, no, that couldn't be... It was just that she hadn't yet completed her mission. She asked, 'Have you received new orders?'

'Not yet. But Karl and Otto are coming over later. They've heard a rumour that we are having a visit from German military intelligence, and they think I would be wise to falsify a few reports. My catch and kill rate is insufficient when it comes to the Resistance, apparently. I confess I've been slack with the deportations, as well. If the Abwehr – or whichever branch of intelligence this is – thinks I'm dragging my feet, it will be off to Russia with me. This French occupation is seen in Berlin as a very cushy way to spend the war, so there are many who would love to see the whole lot of us packed off to the eastern front.'

'But I don't *want* them to send you to Russia...'

He sighed and pulled her closer to him. 'Then let's just keep hoping for the best, shall we? It's all we can do. Everything around us is so uncertain, so there's no point in looking ahead. Only when all of this is over, can we start planning our life together. I'd love to stay here, with you, in France.'

It struck her suddenly, how innocent he was – so young and full of unreasonable hope. His blond hair was cut short in the military style but somehow it didn't manage to make him look austere, only boyish. With an unexpected rush of tenderness, she wound her arms around his neck. 'It's going to be a long fight, I think.'

'Yes. And maybe our enemies will prevail,' he said quietly, his voice barely audible.

'Do you think so?' She prayed her face gave nothing away.

'Things are really heating up. Whatever deal Ribbentrop and Molotov did two years ago, it's well and truly dismantled now. Hitler is determined to smash Stalin, he has always hated him. It's a miracle the truce held as long as it did. Britain still hasn't surrendered, so Germany will be fighting on two fronts. That's what finished the Kaiser in the last war – no army can be overstretched to that extent. Whatever hope Germany has of winning on the western front, the Russians... Let's just say, they are a whole other prospect.'

'You're saying you think that Germany could…' She stopped speaking. She daren't say 'lose'. He might be a more humane man than his grosser colleagues, but he was still a Nazi in every way that mattered.

He glanced around the room as if he feared the walls had ears, then lowered his voice even further. 'I could be shot for saying this. But, yes – I think Germany could lose. And I don't even know what I feel about that.'

His admission hung between them. Catriona rested her cheek on his shoulder, feeling the warmth of his arms around her. Her heart was pounding. Now was her chance – but what should she say? How much should she reveal?

'Is there anything you can do...' she began.

He looked down at her for a long, long moment. Then smiled a flicker of a smile, and said, 'Yes – I can take you back to bed and discuss my love for you at great length.'

'Of course.' Her mind still spinning, she followed him back into the bedroom.

Afterwards she lay in his arms, lost in thought. It was so hard to tell what he was thinking. Did he really hope Germany might lose the war? In which case, why didn't he just come out and say it? But maybe he was like her – maybe he feared that *she* would betray *him*. Should she just take the risk, and tell him who she was? But if she was wrong... She wished that she could consult with Gaston, right then and there.

Reaching across her, Frederik picked up his watch from the bedside locker and groaned. 'I'd better get dressed I suppose. They could be here at any moment.'

'They?'

'Karl and Otto. They're anxious about themselves as well as me, though their rates of success are admittedly much better than mine. Even so, for all of us it's embarrassing here at the moment. The Resistance are growing stronger around Bordeaux and the surrounding Department and we're supposed to be stamping down on them. But they are impossible to detect. It's like trying to catch smoke.'

Turning onto her front, she smothered a smile in the pillow. She knew she had saved a lot of lives, by listening to Frederik's drunken friends. She couldn't help saying, 'You can't blame them though, can you? The French are proud people, and it's humiliating to be occupied.'

He swung his legs out of bed and sat on the edge, saying calmly, 'Blame them? Of course I don't. If I was French, I would most likely be one of them. But I'm not, and so I have to make an effort to capture a few of them, or at least pretend that I have. Look, I'll try to get this matter over within a few hours, and we can have some of the evening together.' He disappeared into the bathroom off their bedroom, calling back to her: 'Do you want to go anywhere? I can have the car brought around to take you for a drive?'

Here was her chance. She called back, 'I would love to visit the vineyard today. I wrote to my mother giving her the vineyard as my address, and maybe she wrote back. I'd like to check.'

'Of course, go.' His head appeared in the doorway, his face covered in shaving cream. 'I'm sure Gaston would keep any mail for you. He is a nice fellow, isn't he? When he invites us to dinner it is as if there is no animosity between our two countries.'

Clearly, he had no idea how deeply Gaston hated the Germans. It was a testament to her uncle's acting abilities that Frederik was totally unaware of how Gaston would, without a moment's hesitation, blow him and all his Nazi colleagues to kingdom come.

'Thank you,' she smiled. 'And I'll be back in time to cook dinner for you and Karl and Otto if you like?'

'That would be wonderful, my darling, I'd really appreciate that.' Moments later, he returned to the bedroom, shaved and washed, and pulled his Nazi uniform out of the wardrobe.

Sitting in her negligée on the edge of the bed, she watched him dress. Sometimes, she was glad to see him in that hateful uniform. It helped to draw a line between them. Frederik on one side, oppressing her countrymen; she on the other side, trying to free them.

The bell rang and he strode away down the hall. The other

two must be here. She dressed slowly and went down to greet them in the office, where Frederik and Otto were standing at the table pouring over a communiqué from Berlin.

'Ah the lovely Emilie!' Fat, stocky Karl rose from the leather armchair where he was sitting smoking, and waddled to embrace her. He held her a little too long and much too tightly. She tried not to shudder.

'How nice to see you again,' she said demurely in German, before turning to Otto. 'Otto, you look so much better, and has that cold cleared up?' She had feigned concern over his coughing the last time he was here, and had given him a hot whiskey made with lemon and cloves and brown sugar – Kieran's typically Irish cure-all.

'Ah yes, that magic potion you made me worked a treat, though now I fear I have a new addiction. You must show me how to make it.'

'Cigarette, Emilie?' Karl was trying to recapture her attention, waving a cigarette in her face. Politely, she accepted it and inclined her head. He pulled a solid silver lighter from his pocket, and flicked it open with his thumb.

Catriona's stomach lurched and without thinking, she put her hand on his thick, hairy wrist to stop him moving the flame away. He looked at her with a lecherous grin, and she recovered herself enough to say, 'Wait, *encore*… My cigarette is not lit properly.'

'Of course.' Winking at her – clearly enjoying the touch of her hand on his – he flicked the lighter again. His fat thumb covered most of the inscription, but she could make out the word *'aujourd'hui'*, and beneath it: *'plus qu'hier'.* She'd been right. It was her father's lighter. His precious, irreplaceable lighter – his last gift from Eloise, which he never let out of his sight.

She inhaled. 'Thank you, Karl. What a beautiful lighter

you have there.' She hoped her voice sounded steady and normal.

'You like my… *lighter?'* He flushed coarsely – bright red.

She shivered. 'I do.'

'Then you have excellent taste,' he grinned, with a slight nod of his head – his hand rested on her waist unnecessarily before she moved deftly aside.

She made small talk while she finished her cigarette, French women did not smoke in public, and she stubbed it out on the heavy onyx ashtray that had been in the apartment since they moved in. So many objects, owned presumably by the previous inhabitants, remained and she tried not to think where those people were now.

'Goodbye, everyone.' She went to kiss Frederik on the cheek, then – with a smile on her lips and grief in her heart – she gathered her bag, hat and gloves, and left the apartment.

CHAPTER 8

Passing through the vineyard of Chateau de Clairand she greeted two of the women with whom she'd worked in the early days. They refused to speak to her, turning their backs as she passed. It was unsurprising – yet still it hurt. As far as all these women were concerned, she was no better than the females who worked the docks and gave themselves to the Germans. In fact, they probably thought the prostitutes were more honest.

Reaching the chateau, she first twisted the ancient weather vane as Gaston had taught her – casually, as if playing with the rusty old thing – then rang the bell. A young servant girl opened the door and showed her into the conservatory. Like the women in the vineyard, the girl radiated animosity – wrinkling her nose as if she had smelled something foul.

Loic appeared in the conservatory about ten minutes later.

'Ah Emilie, how nice to see you.' He greeted her with a kiss on each cheek, carrying on the pretence that she was a former employee and now the girlfriend of their friendly neighbourhood German officer. 'My father told me you were here and perhaps wished to speak to someone.'

'I just wondered if any letters had come for me, but your housemaid says no. I was hoping to hear from my mother.' She stood and moved towards the glass doors overlooking the gently undulating vineyards below. 'The whole estate is looking so lovely, would you mind if we took a walk?' She had been told in London that when she had information to impart it was always safer to do it out in the open, where there was less chance of being overheard.

He understood at once. 'I'm sorry we have no letter for you. But since you've come all this way, of course, let me show you around. They are leaf-thinning at the moment to ensure the grapes get enough sunlight to sweeten, but one must watch for overly enthusiastic pruners. My father nearly went mad last week when some of the new people thinned too much and the grapes got burned.' He ushered her out of the doors.

Once they were clear of the house and yard, and surrounded by vines, she changed her tone and said earnestly, 'Loic, remember Karl Fischer, that loathsome fat German officer who works with Frederik?'

Her cousin nodded.

'He has my father's lighter. Oh Loic…' She could barely say the words. 'I think…'

'I understand.' All traces of earlier levity disappeared from Loic's manner. 'Look, make a big show of saying goodbye to me now, though I don't think anyone is watching, then go to the yard. The driver is being fed by the cook so he won't look for you and everyone else is out at the vines. Go in by the lilac tree. He'll come to you shortly.'

She smiled and kissed his cheeks, and waved as she walked away from him, forcing herself to stop and admire the vines as she went. She even paused to smell the fragrant rose planted at the end of the row of vines. She always loved to see the roses in bloom and thought they looked so romantic, although her uncle was quick to point out how the roses were not there for their beauty but as an early warning of mildew or fungus growing on his vines.

She passed around the house, managed to make her way unseen to the lilac tree, found the spare key, checked that she still wasn't being observed and let herself into the cellar.

She waited for over twenty minutes in the damp dark cave, desperate for Gaston to come. She paced and worried and tried to think what it all meant. The obvious thing was that Karl had killed her father and taken his lighter. And Karl was Frederik's colleague, so surely Frederik must know that Kieran was dead. Or did he? He had sounded so genuine when he talked about looking Kieran up in Ireland, if indeed his Irish friend *was* actually Kieran… Round and round it all went. Should she just confront him, demanding the truth? Or was that reckless?

She felt like screaming.

Light footsteps approached, as if on tiptoe, and she shrank into the back of the cave. Then someone turned on the single bulb… and it was not Gaston, but her grandmother. 'Gaston thought you might need me, Catriona?'

'Oh Mémé, yes I do…' The sight of her grandmother released all the emotions that Catriona had been keeping under such close watch since seeing her father's lighter in Karl's clumsy fist. With a cry of pent-up grief, she rushed into Louise's comforting arms. Her grandmother stroked her back and let her cry.

'The Nazis have his lighter. But that doesn't mean he's dead, Mémé, does it?' she sobbed. 'I mean Karl could have stolen it from him... Please Mémé, say something...' She knew she sounded childish but she was so distraught. 'He is all I have.'

Louise tightened her thin arms around her granddaughter. 'Catriona, I know you love your father, of course you do, and I realise now he was a truly wonderful man. But, remember this: he is not all you have in the world. You have me and Pépé and Gaston and Marie-Clare and Loic. You might be Irish, but in here…' Mémé stepped back and pointed to Catriona's heart, '…in here, you are French as well. We are your family, Catriona.'

'We are your family,' echoed a second voice, and it was Gaston. He also embraced her. 'My poor Catriona.'

She hugged him back briefly, then took a deep breath. Whatever the truth about her father, now was not the time to collapse. She had to stay focused. 'Mémé, may I speak with Gaston alone again? It's how I've been told to do things.'

As before, her grandmother was reluctant to leave, and clung to her: 'Everything is so very dangerous, and these Boche, they will stop at nothing...'

Catriona gently ushered her towards the door. Her grandmother seized her hand, not wanting to let her go. Catriona almost wished she wouldn't. Any further show of love and care would only serve to weaken her again. 'I know you are worried about me, Mémé….'

'If the Germans were to find out who you are, and arrest you... I'm so afraid. They're getting stronger, they are winning on the eastern front, new victories every day, taking more and more Russian prisoners to drive their war production. Rumour has it that Churchill and Roosevelt are offering to help Russia – did we ever think we'd see this day? – but I fear it won't be enough.'

'Then don't try to stop me in my work, Mémé. I love you so much and to know I have a loving family here, it means so much to me. But I am doing this with my eyes wide open. These monsters probably killed my father, they're enslaving my family and destroying the country I think of as my second home, so I *want* to do this.'

'Oh Catriona...'

'Au revoir, Mémé. Je t'aime.'

After her grandmother had been persuaded to leave, Catriona turned to Gaston and said quickly, 'I've not just come to tell you about my father. Karl and Otto are with Frederik today. Investigators are coming from Berlin, from military intelligence, to crack down on Frederik for being too weak in combating the Resistance around Bordeaux.'

Gaston looked alarmed. 'Who is coming? Who are they?'

'I don't know their names or rank, but I will try to find out. They are from the Abwehr, I think. Although there are so many agencies working here now – the Geheime Feldpolizei, the Abwehr, the Gestapo, not to mention all the branches of the military administration. Frederik says there are too many people trying to do the same job and they are only getting in each other's way.'

Gaston nodded. 'Things are becoming much more intense. Some resister was shot and killed – a Communist, I think – in Strasbourg and it's led to all sorts of reprisals. It is drawing a lot of unwanted attention on us here. And Pétain is dancing like a little puppet to Hitler's tune, saying he put an end to mutiny in 1917 and he'll do the same now. Apparently, he is trying to save us from ourselves, the stupid traitorous fool... People are so demoralised, feeling like there is nothing we can do. Our government has failed us miserably and people are afraid for the future. If only we can show people that we can fight back, then they will be emboldened to join us and maybe together we can free our country.'

'I agree. I'll find out exactly who these investigators are and I'll pass it on to Fabien,' she paused, an idea just occurring to her. 'If we can do something, something big, something that cannot go unnoticed, either here or in Berlin, then the people will see what the Resistance is capable of.'

'You're right, but we don't have the resources or the opportunity to inflict much pain on the Germans.' Gaston sighed and shrugged.

'You don't need much in the way of resources when the enemy are sitting at your dining room table.' Catriona said slowly, the idea forming in her mind.

Gaston looked at her intently, his face at first registering shock but then something else. 'You're thinking, we should kill these investigators?'

'Yes, in fact we must.' She was almost shocked at how determined she felt. She wanted revenge for what these brutes were doing to France, and – just as much as that – she wanted justice for Kieran. 'I'm not naïve. I know Berlin will just send more Germans to replace them. But it will raise French morale and that is what's necessary, you said so yourself. It will inspire confidence in others to act, and join us. With more members we could make operating here so difficult for the Germans, to the point of impossible, then we could just turn the tide of this war.'

He put his hand on her shoulder. 'Good girl. You're right. Invite them to dinner, get them drunk, and we'll burst in with grenades and kill them all.'

'No.' She thought carefully. 'Too risky. A bomb would be better. Somewhere they would never think to find it.' An idea occurred to her based on a class on explosives she'd taken in London. A bomb can be placed in anything. 'I know, I'll cook a goose for their dinner, and put the charge inside its neck – plastic explosive and some pencil detonators which I can set on a timer.'

Gaston wasn't convinced. 'You can do this?'

'Yes, I did some work with detonators in the month I was

in Baker Street. A cell being run from England is operating here, is it not? Maybe they will have explosives to give us.'

'Ah yes, the English always have their own people…' Gaston rolled his eyes. 'Too many factions, all wanting the same thing but each operating on their own. It can't go on. Anyway, not your problem. If you're sure, I will make contact with someone who can get us what we need.'

'I'm sure. Also, we must make sure there is nobody else in the building. It is three storeys high with shops either side which will be empty by evening, but the woman downstairs has children, and they must be out. The other flat is empty, so it's just her and the concierge.' Catriona always said hello to the heavy-set widow if she bumped into her entering or leaving the building but the woman never answered, neither did the octogenarian half-deaf concierge. No doubt, they saw Catriona as a German collaborator and wanted nothing to do with her.

He nodded. 'We'll see to that. We can't say or do anything to arouse suspicion but someone will say something at the last moment.'

'Thank you.' She didn't want to be responsible for the loss of any French lives.

'And we will arrange to have you picked up immediately afterwards, and get you lifted out. We will ensure the wireless operator gets a message to London, and nobody on the German side will look for you. They'll assume you were killed in the blast.' He paced the cellar floor as he thought aloud: 'The grenades can be back up. As soon as we see you leave the apartment, we'll be ready to rush the place in case the bomb doesn't go off. Six Nazis taken out in one fell swoop… '

Catriona's chest tightened, at the thought of Frederik being murdered along with his colleagues. For a moment she couldn't speak. She knew Gaston strongly suspected Frederik of betraying Kieran. And yet…

'What?' Gaston was looking at her closely. 'What's the matter?'

'Frederik…' She hesitated.

'What about Schroeder?'

'He is growing increasingly disillusioned, Gaston. I think London may be right, and he is ready to be turned. He thinks Germany will lose. I'm sure he despises Hitler. Should I tell him about the lighter, and see his reaction? Maybe that will be enough to bring him in and if we can do that before these men come from Berlin…'

Gaston ran his hands through his thick mop of hair, and exhaled slowly. 'No. It's too big a risk.'

'It's what London asked me to do.'

'But if they tortured you…'

'I have the cyanide pill.'

He shuddered. 'Don't think about that.'

'My father believed Frederik was ready to turn. London trusts my father's opinion. They wanted me to finish my father's work.'

'Ah Catriona. Those people in London don't love you as your family do. They see you merely as a useful tool in the war…'

'Maybe so, but if I die, I will have died doing something I believe in. Please, let me try to recruit him to our side.' She did her best to keep any feelings she might have developed for Frederik out of her voice, but Gaston's face darkened.

'Catriona, if you're mistaken… Frederik knows of the connection between you and this place, and so will realise who we are. My wife, my son, your grandparents. No, there is too much at stake. Not only you, but none of them will be safe if this goes wrong.'

'Then if necessary, I'll kill him before he can raise the

alarm.' She caught her breath, hardly believing herself capable of saying such words. Gaston leant his back against the cool stone wall, arms crossed, looking intently at her.

'Do you really think you can do that?'

Catriona felt her cheeks redden, as she realised that her uncle had seen more than she had imagined. 'Of course. He's the enemy and...'

'Catriona,' he interrupted her. 'I'm sure it's hard, in the circumstances, not to develop... certain feelings. So I'll ask you again. Are you sure you can shoot Frederik?'

'I'll do it for Kieran and for all of you,' she said firmly.

His face was impassive. 'How?'

'He leaves his gun in the dressing room. I'll insist we go on a picnic, complain that I never see him these days because he's so busy with work and I'll bring it in my leather camera case. I'll tell him who I am when we are walking in the forest, far from listening ears. And if he reacts badly, I'll shoot him. You can get a message to London that I need to be picked up, and I'll go back to England and there won't be any repercussions for you.'

He nodded, satisfied. 'Then I trust you.' He pulled her into his embrace again. 'We all love you Catriona, and I know what my dear sister would say if she saw you now. That she loves you too. You are a remarkable young woman, and your family – and your country – are so proud of your bravery.'

'Vive la France,' she whispered, and pulled away from him before she could weaken and break down in tears.

* * *

THE DRIVER WAS WAITING in the car. He was a young literature student from Bavaria, reading a book, happily full from the chateau's legendary quiche Lorraine and pommes frites.

'Fräulein!' He shot to attention. 'Excuse me...I...' He leapt out and raced around the car to open the passenger door for her.

'Please don't worry, Hans, it's fine,' she reassured him, as she sat in. As he returned to the driver's seat, she looked back at the chateau. Would she ever see it again? Her gaze was drawn to the lower drawing room window – where her grandmother and her uncle stood, watching her. Gaston had his huge hand on his mother's small bony shoulder, and the sight of such tenderness stung Catriona's eyes. These were her people, not Frederik – she would remember that and do what she had to. As the car inched around the large turning circle in front of the chateau, her grandmother raised her fingers to her lips and kissed them, then pressed them to the glass.

Catriona mimicked her grandmother's gesture: kissing her fingertips and touching them to the passenger window. A moment of shared love, and then the vision was gone.

CHAPTER 9

'Emilie, have you seen that file, the buff coloured one I left on the dining room table last night? Karl and Otto will be here any moment…' Frederik was harassed. This visitation from the Abwehr was really rattling him. 'I left it there, I'm sure of it.' He ran his fingers through his cropped blond hair.

'Frederik, I'll find the report for you – but please, can you just take a couple of hours off? I know you are very worried about this inspection, but honestly, these days you don't sleep, you hardly eat, and Otto and Karl are here all the time, always hassling you. Tell them to stay away!'

'I need them, Emilie. They are helping me with these reports. I've been lax, I have let people go, I have turned a blind eye. I've been falsifying papers, issuing travel permits to people who shouldn't have them, inflating deportation numbers, writing reports on interrogations that never took place. I'm a dead man unless they back me up and cover for me…' He was pale and dishevelled.

She begged, 'Just take this one single afternoon off. It will be the first time we've been alone for days. We could go out to La Forêt des Landes, walk in the woods, maybe take some pictures with my camera.' She tried to hold his hands, to prevent him moving away from her.

He shuddered. 'Emilie darling, I can't.'

She wrapped her arms around his waist. He'd gotten thin with anxiety. 'No. I've made my decision. I'm packing a picnic for us, and we're going. We will take two hours, not a moment more, but you need a break.' She pulled him closer. 'Please.'

She was determined to get him alone, out in the open where they could not be overheard. She had already made up the picnic basket. Cheese, baguettes, ham, red wine. She'd packed the leather case of her expensive camera. And his gun, in the leather case. If they were in the middle of the forest, no-one but Frederik could possibly hear what she had to say. Or hear what he might choose to answer.

Or hear the gun shot, if she had to shoot him.

He pulled away. 'Emilie, you are possibly the only good thing in my life, and going for a walk with you – in fact, walking off into the sunset with you forever and ever – sounds the most appealing prospect I could imagine...'

'Then please. Please come with me. It's important.'

'No, I'm sorry, but if these henchmen of the Führer figure out that I'm not doing my job as enthusiastically as I should be doing it, they will delight in sending me to the Eastern front. So I simply can't run off with you, not even for a minute.'

As he moved away, still in search of the folder, she heard herself say: 'I'm Kieran McCarthy's daughter.'

He stopped dead. Spun to face her. All the colour draining from his face. 'What did you just say?' He covered the distance between them in two strides.

She shrunk back against the wall and gasped out, 'I'm not

Emilie, I'm Catriona McCarthy, and I'm here to find out what happened to my father.'

Saying nothing, he seized her and hustled her down the hallway into the bedroom, pushed her onto the bed and slammed and locked the door. She sat huddled with her knees pressed against the bedside locker as he closed the curtains. This was a disaster. She had misjudged him. The picnic basket was in the kitchen – with the gun. She had sentenced all the de Clairands to death.

'Frederik,' she pleaded. 'I beg you, let me go and make us some coffee while we talk about this quietly…'

'No,' he snarled, standing with his back pressed to the door. 'Talk to me right here. In our bedroom. Who are you?'

She did her best to keep her voice calm and steady. 'I told you. My name is Catriona McCarthy, and I'm Kieran McCarthy's daughter.'

'You're a *spy.*' He spat out the word. She flinched at the venom in his voice. She'd never heard that in him before.

'I didn't mean to hurt you, Frederik. I just wanted to find out what happened to my father…'

'Who was a spy as well. Don't try to pretend you don't know that. He was trying to recruit me before he suddenly disappeared back to London. Now I think about it, probably he thought we'd been overheard and he ran away and left me to be shot as a traitor.'

'No, no, he wouldn't do that!' she gasped, horrified. 'He thought you were a good man. He told the people in London that he trusted you!'

'Well then maybe he thought you'd do a better job with me than he could because you could give me something he couldn't give me. Oh Emilie...' His face crumpled into abject misery and his voice cracked.

'I'm Catriona,' she whispered.

'Catriona... Oh God.' He clutched his arms across his chest, and squeezed his eyes shut with pain. 'This can't be happening. In all this crazy horrible mess, you were the only thing that made my life worthwhile, and now… This was a set up from the start, wasn't it? Me meeting you, you moving in here.'

She hated to hear the agony in his voice. "Yes, it was, but I… What I feel for you now is real...'

He made an angry, dismissive gesture. 'Why on earth should I believe you? You're trained to get what you want, to pick your target and do whatever it takes, even if that means doing it on your back.' He cast her a look of deep contempt. 'You look down on the girls who roam the quays at night, but you're no better. You were so sure I'd fall for your lies and come running like a puppy into your arms, weren't you? When I met you at Chateau de Clairand...' His blue eyes widened. The truth was dawning on him. 'I thought Gaston was my friend, and he was in on this all the time!'

She dug her nails into the palms of her hands to keep herself from panicking. The gun was in the kitchen. All she could do was lay all her cards on the table, and hope he was the man she thought he was, in his heart. 'You're right. Gaston is my uncle. My mother was his sister.'

He groaned, 'Oh God…' and buried his face in his hands.

She stepped towards him. Just a single step. 'Frederik, listen to me. Together we can do our bit to make sure this evil regime is stopped. We can do this, together. I have connections, just as my father did. We can escape, go to London. We can get airlifted out back to England, both of us. You would be of such use to them there, with all you know.'

He raised his head; his eyes were bloodshot and his cropped hair was standing on end. 'Oh God, this is madness. The Abwehr, the bloody Abwehr are coming here, to this apartment, in three days' time. They will be dining here in this place, with us, and you think I can just jump over to the British side? Are you insane?'

Her heart lifted, just a little. He hadn't refused – only said it was madness. 'I'm not insane – and nor are you. You hate Hitler. Work with me. Work with us, like my father wanted you to do. Germany is going to lose the war, and we can help make that happen sooner. Think of all the suffering that people will be spared, if the war is over. All the lives that will be saved. Help me.'

He clenched his fists, shaking his head in an agony of indecision. 'I do hate Hitler and everything he stands for, but what you are asking me to do, it's not just to betray Hitler, it's to betray my country.'

'Isn't France your country too? Think of your mother.'

'You're asking me to betray my friends!'

She took another step towards him. 'Karl and Otto are not your friends. Karl murdered my father and never told you.'

He jerked back, shocked. 'No, that can't be true. Karl told me that he saw Kieran McCarthy get on the train to Paris.'

'Karl lied to you. Five days ago, he lit my cigarette with Kieran's own lighter. It was my father's most treasured possession. My mother gave it to him just before she died and he never, ever let it out of his sight.' She was doing her best not to cry but the tears came anyway.

For a moment she wept alone, with Frederick staring blankly at her. But when he spoke, it was with a tone of resignation in his voice she'd not heard before.

'I swear, Emi… Catriona. I knew none of this about your father. If he was picked up and transported or even worse, then neither Karl nor Otto ever mentioned anything about it. If you're right and Karl did this without my knowledge and Otto covered for him…'

She turned her tear-stained face to look at him. Without

meeting her eyes, he leaned past her to his locker and took out his packet of cigarettes, lit one and settled beside her on his back. He blew out a long stream of cigarette smoke, before he finished his sentence:

'…well then, they know everything, and both of us are in terrible danger.'

For a long while they lay together, not touching, as the sun shone through the thin curtains. At last, she raised herself on one elbow, gazing down into his face. 'Who is coming here from the Abwehr?' she asked.

He shrugged, glancing at her. 'I don't know the names, but they will not be office boys. There is very bad blood between the Abwehr and the SS, and the SS are close to Berlin, so the Abwehr must be keen to raise their own profile by finding a rogue officer – like me. Otto let slip last night that these visitors have a directive from Canaris himself, which could well have come from Hitler – who knows? The more I think about it, this is not a random investigation. No, they are coming for me, and that's that. Karl has tipped them off, and Otto is playing along.' He sat up suddenly and stubbed out his cigarette in the ashtray beside the bed, saying bitterly, 'It makes sense, Emi… Catriona. It all makes horrible sense. Oh God, what are we going to do?'

She also sat up, cross-legged on the bed, and gazed at him with steely determination. 'Wipe them out. We have to kill them before they kill us.'

'What?' He went white.

'We'll invite them here for dinner, on the night they arrive. Karl and Otto will be here as well. The Resistance need to feel that they are getting somewhere. The reprisals, the directives, the threats are terrifying people into submission, making them believe that Hitler is winning. If we could do this, it would be a victory for the Resistance, and five fewer Nazis in the world.'

He stared at her incredulously. 'You're serious.' A statement, not a question. 'You want me to invite them to dinner and then… murder them? It's…horrific.'

Her gaze never left his face. 'This is war, and in war, you cannot be clouded by sentiment. Karl and Otto have betrayed you. These men are coming for you, and they'll send you to Russia and replace you with some Nazi who will send more people to the camps, have more French men and women deported and killed, impose harsher and harsher sanctions on the starving population. We may not get an opportunity like this again. We have to take it.'

'Oh God…'

'Listen to me, Frederik. We're the same you and I. Not especially brave or anything but here we are, in this time and place and we have a chance to do something good, something really meaningful. Can't you see we have no choice? Everything we love, our freedom, everything is at stake here. You can't just hide. You have to decide which side of history you want to be on. The side of evil, death and destruction with them, or the side of decency and right, with me?'

Her gaze never left his face, and she saw the raw conflict there in his youthful eyes. She took his hand and held it.

'I love you, Frederik. I'm not saying that to convince you, I genuinely love you and I want all the things we've talked about, for us to get married, have a family, grow old together. But that can never happen under Hitler. It's very dangerous what I'm proposing, I am well aware of it, but I have to fight back. We all have to. Otherwise what is there for any of us in the future?'

With a shiver, he lifted his hand towards her cheek – but it wasn't until he'd wiped the tear from her face that she realised she had been crying.

'Do you swear you love me?' he asked softly. 'I'm not just a project, someone to recruit?'

In response, Catriona said words that she had never uttered before: 'I swear on my parents' lives that I love you.'

Shaking his head in wonder, he drew her into his arms and they lay down together on the bed, in silence. She rested her head on his chest, listening to his heart beating, longing to know what he was thinking but knowing him well enough now to believe he would tell her the right answer, in his own time.

CHAPTER 10

The apartment smelled invitingly of lilies, grown at the chateau by her grandmother and delivered via the café. Everything was perfectly arranged. The aperitif tray sat on the sideboard, the crystal glasses glinting in the sun through the open balcony windows.

A huge goose – also supplied by the chateau – was roasting in the oven and because it was so warm, Catriona had opted to serve it with bread and salads rather than vegetables. Gaston had supplied the wine and she knew the Germans would be impressed. They would be less so if they knew what else he had supplied for the evening: she had a tiny Walther 6.35mm caliber semi automatic pistol, liberated from a German by the Resistance no doubt, strapped to the inside of her thigh, fully loaded. Gaston assured her that while it was small, it would do the job if needed.

Frederik was also carrying his gun. Catriona had returned it to his bedside drawer without his ever having noticed that it had gone missing, sparing her having to admit that she had ever planned to shoot him. Warmth filled her heart at the thought of her handsome lover – it was wonderful, how he had agreed to change sides and strike a blow for France before heading for London.

Right now, he was at the train station with Karl and Otto, picking up the three Abwehr agents before bringing them straight back to the apartment, where he would serve aperitifs on the balcony before the meal, doing his best to get as much alcohol into the five Nazis as possible.

Luckily, the configuration of the apartment suited their plan for the evening perfectly. The dining room was to the left of the front door, a lovely sunny space overlooking the river below, while the kitchen was at the back of the apartment. The bathroom was nearer to the dining room than the kitchen, so there was no reason for anyone but she or Frederik to approach the kitchen. Just to be safe however, the ingredients for the bomb were hidden in the pantry. Supplies were very precious so a dry run was not an option, but she knew the explosive and timing pencils had come in a drop from London relatively recently and would have been tested there. She knew what to do – she had been trained in Baker Street. It wasn't hard. Just risky.

She hoped Loic had already ensured that the other inhabitants of the building were gone – the widow and her children, and the concierge. She knew other members of the Resistance would be close by, ready to act on Gaston's backup plan. She prayed it wouldn't be necessary. She didn't want any of her French countrymen to risk their lives today.

Fabien's cousin Yves would be waiting in a car to get herself and Frederik out of the city. Very few cars were running these days because petrol was close to impossible to come by, but Yves was a doctor so he was allowed a small amount of fuel. Catriona's instructions were to get to the corner of Place des Bourges and Place Jean Jaurès, where Yves would be parked, and from there he would take her and Frederik to the outskirts of the city. There they would be met by someone else – she didn't know who – and brought to a field where a plane would come to collect them.

There were so many parts to the plan, she thought, and if any single one of them went wrong... She stopped herself. That was counterproductive – they were in it now up to their necks either way, and it was going to have to be done.

Her heart thumped violently as she heard Frederik's key in the door, and his voice inviting everyone out onto the balcony for aperitifs. Catriona had made a summer punch based on her grandmother's infamous recipe that would knock out a horse, but which somehow still tasted light and summery. The secret was to use elderflower cordial and a fairly tasteless *eau de vie* along with plenty of other spirits to make it more potent. It was delicious, but after a glass or two most people were distinctly woozy.

She removed her apron and went into the bedroom. Everything was just so; nothing out of place and if all went well, in a little over an hour all that would remain was rubble. Gaston had assured her that the British had erred on the side of caution and there was enough explosive to take out the entire building. It was a shame – it was a beautiful piece of architecture – but like so many other things, it was going to have to be sacrificed for the good of her people. It could be rebuilt by the French themselves, once they were free.

She stood in front of the mirror. Was she the same girl that had left the nuns nearly three years ago, knowing nothing of the world? She tried hard to remember that care-free, cheeky schoolgirl, always up to some kind of mischief. Was she gone for good? She had no idea, but the hardened person she was now was nothing like her old self.

Still, she'd managed to look young and fresh. She wore a red dress that cinched in at the waist and flared into a full skirt, and revealed a lot more cleavage than the ones she usually wore – but her job was to charm the visitors into relaxing. Her blonde hair had been coiffed in the hair salon this morning, into soft waves that framed her face, and her dark brown eyes were round and clear.

She took a deep breath and said a silent prayer.

'Dear God, and Maman and Kieran if you're up there, please look after us tonight, and let us get out of here alive. I'm not sorry for what I'm about to do though I know to take another life is a mortal sin, but I'm doing it so innocent lives might be spared. If you can, please watch over us. I love you.'

It was time.

Frederik was already serving the punch when she appeared on the balcony. Otto and Karl greeted her warmly – Karl's eyes being drawn to her cleavage as she'd expected. He had a wife back in Dusseldorf but she was never mentioned, unlike Otto who never stopped going on about his own wife Cristiana and his children. Their apartment in Berlin had taken a direct hit last week. As he'd confided in Catriona during one of his almost daily visits, 'being bombed by the British was one thing, but the Russians are coming for us now. Berlin is getting a hammering like nothing we've seen before. My wife is trying to get to her parents' place near Munich but I don't know if she can. My children are only seven and five, and we've lost everything in the explosion, and there is nothing I can do...' He had sighed heavily, but had allowed Catriona to comfort him with another hot whiskey.

Frederik introduced her to the first of the three men she didn't recognise: 'Emilie, this is Rudolf Becker.'

She shook his hand. Dark hair, average height and build, pale blue eyes, instantly forgettable. He wasn't even wearing uniform. Frederik had explained that the Abwehr mainly wore civilian clothes; while some of them held a military rank, they did not use it when operating as agents.

'Good evening, Herr Becker. It's a pleasure to have you here.'

He smiled, and shook her hand. 'You speak excellent German,' he remarked in a smooth, soft voice that she found chilling.

'I'm Belgian and I went to school in the German-speaking part of Belgium so I am bilingual, and my best school friend Trudi was from Frankfurt.'

'Are you still in touch?' he asked.

'Alas, no. I wrote but got no reply.'

'Perhaps when the war is over, you will meet her again.' Catriona got the impression that reuniting old friends was not what this conversation was about. He was testing her loyalties.

'I certainly hope so,' she smiled sweetly. 'I liked her very much.'

Frederik moved her on to the next visitor. 'Let me introduce Albert Hoffman. You are from Aachen, are you not, Albert?' he asked pleasantly.

Albert was in his sixties, she guessed, with brushed-back silver hair and a neat moustache. He was short and dapper and perfectly dressed in a double-breasted suit. A blood-red handkerchief was folded in his breast pocket, which matched his tie.

'Yes, that's right. Have you been to Aachen, Fräulein?' He sipped his punch, and his tone was light and pleasant.

'Oh yes, many times. One of the nuns was enthralled by the collections at the Suermondt Museum, so we visited regularly. Though to be honest, the best part for us was enjoying hot chocolate and pretzels in Café Brigitta on Peterstrasse.' She laughed and Albert laughed with her.

'Ah yes, Café Brigitta, I can still recall the aroma as we walked past her café. My grandmother lived near there and my mother would forbid us to eat anything before lunch at

Grandma's in case we insulted her by not clearing our plates, but the temptation was enormous. It is nice to meet you, Fräulein.'

Frederik moved her on again. 'And finally, this is Bruno Neumann.'

'Fräulein,' he nodded, but he did not take her outstretched hand. He was the only one of those present not to be holding a drink.

She lowered her hand. 'You're most welcome, Herr Neumann. Would you like some punch?'

'No.'

'Can I get you something else if the punch is not to your taste?'

'No.' He lacked any social graces whatsoever, clearly caring nothing that he came across as rude.

He was tall and powerfully built, his hair so short it was almost shaved. He moved stiffly and stood with his back to them, observing life on the quayside below. Karl offered his silver cigarette case around, and everyone but Neumann refused. Karl reached into his pocket and Catriona braced herself to see her father's silver lighter again. Sure enough, out it came. She ached to grab it from him. Instead, she nailed a smile on her face and joined in the small talk: life back in Berlin; the progress of the war; the genius of *der Führer*, how they were giving the Russians a right trouncing. Neumann didn't engage at all, just stood watching the street below and smoking.

After half an hour of excruciating small talk, Catriona excused herself, saying she needed to attend to matters in the kitchen. The goose was cooked and she was taking it out of the oven to rest before carving when she heard footsteps in the passageway. Her heart missed a beat.

Calm down, she commanded herself silently – *there is nothing incriminating to see in here.*

When she turned, it was Karl.

'Emilie, do you need any help?' he asked, his smile lecherous.

'No thank you, Karl, everything is under control,' she replied as coolly as she could manage.

He entered the kitchen and kicked the door closed behind him with his foot. Suddenly she was cornered and he was so close she could smell the cigarette smoke on his breath.

'You're very pretty, you know,' he began, running a finger down her cheek, 'but I'm not falling for that innocent little girl act. Why are you hiding from me?' He reminded her of the wolf in the storybook she'd had as a child about Little Red Riding Hood. *What did he mean, hiding? Did he know something?* She fought back the panic.

'Of course I wasn't hiding from you ...'

He grinned and put his arms around her waist, roughly pulling her towards him. 'Good. Because I can protect you, Emilie. I fear it's Russia for poor old Frederik – they know about him being too soft here, and even nearly being duped by a British spy, the fool. But I'll be staying after he goes and a nice girl like you...' He glanced around the kitchen '...and a nice apartment like this, come to think of it, would suit me perfectly.'

'Karl, go back to the others – I need to prepare the meal.' She shoved at his chest, trying to give herself some breathing space, but he tightened his grip, delighted.

'That's more like it! I have imagined you so often as a little vixen, fighting back. I'd love that, you and me, biting and scratching...' His face was in her neck, and she could feel his teeth touching her skin. His hand snuck up her dress and he squeezed the back of her thigh, within millimetres of the concealed pistol. She had to act – now.

'Get off me!' she hissed and raised her knee as forcefully

as she could, catching him right in the crotch and causing him to instantly release her and double over in pain.

'You little bi...' he choked out, but before he could finish the word, the door opened and Frederik put his head around it.

'Everything alright in here?' he asked, staring at Karl.

'Yes, wonderful. Karl was just on his way back to you all,' she sang brightly as the red-faced Karl reluctantly and painfully straightened himself. 'Dinner will be served in ten minutes.'

'Thank you, darling.' Frederik waited for Karl to pass in front of him, then – after throwing a startled glance at Catriona – followed him back into the apartment.

After she had recovered her breath, Catriona delivered platters of charcuterie and bowls of salads to the table in the dining room and decanted two bottles of the '36. It was not as good as the '37, which Gaston said would only be drunk when France was free once more, but it was a very good vintage nonetheless – much better than he normally wasted on Germans.

Then she moved out onto the balcony. Karl was nowhere to be seen and the others were talking intently, with their backs to her. There appeared to be a tense atmosphere now, and the jovial chit chat of earlier was notable by its absence. She spotted Karl's cigarettes with the lighter on the side table beside the now empty punch bowl. Quickly she slipped the lighter into her bra, under her arm.

The men stopped talking and turned when she lifted her voice: 'Dinner is served, gentlemen!'

Taking their seats at the large oval table, the visitors returned to idle chatter and – with the exception of Neumann – exclaimed in delight at the vast array of delicacies on display. Albert unfolded his napkin and admired the feast with slightly drunken relish. 'Ha! These French would have you believe they are half-starved but look at this fine spread. Thank you, my dear!'

'It's my pleasure, sir,' Catriona smiled.

Frederik rubbed his hands together. 'Eat and drink your fill, gentlemen. It is such an honour to have you here.'

Karl – who had just emerged shakily from the direction of the bathroom to take his seat at the table – needed no second bidding: he was already pouring himself a large glass.

Catriona headed for the door. 'Please excuse me, I must get the centrepiece.'

'Do you need some help?' asked Frederik. They had thought of this previously – surely one of the men would offer to lift the heavy bird to the table, so it was better that he offered and she refused.

'Not at all, Frederik, it's not heavy and I have a few finishing touches I need to put to the garnish. I'll be back in a moment.'

She retreated to the kitchen and closed the door behind her and set to work.

The explosive was packed and cut into pieces small enough to fit into the neck of the bird. Working at speed, the way she'd been shown in London, she bound four blocks together. She then took the timing pencil, cracked the glass vial with a rolling pin and, once she was sure the acid could escape and corrode the wire, she stuck it into the explosive, inside the bird. She carefully arranged the flaps of fat from the neck to conceal the opening and sprinkled some sprigs of parsley and sage. The whole process had taken her less than a minute. Now they had maybe five minutes until the bomb went off – six at the most. Her heart was racing and sweat prickled on her forehead and back.

The kitchen door opened and she spun around, terrified it was Karl returned to finish what he tried to start. It was

Frederik. She experienced a split second of relief before she realised he was shaking.

'What's wrong?' she whispered, trying not to panic.

He closed the door softly behind him. His eyes were wild. 'I've made a decision. We can't do this, Catriona.'

Her brain span. 'Do what? I don't understa...'

He crossed the kitchen, taking her hands in his. His palms were cold and sweaty, and he was trembling from head to foot. 'I don't want you to set the bomb.'

'What?'

'Shh. Don't say anything. Just listen to me.' His blue eyes pleaded with hers. 'Listen to me. I love you, and I want to run away with you and save myself and be happy. But I can't do this to my own people. They are my fellow countrymen, they are fathers, husbands, it's wrong...'

She couldn't believe this was happening. She tried to pull away from him. 'No, no... I thought you were on my side! You said you...'

He gripped her hands tighter. 'I *am* on your side, *meine liebling* – yours and mine. Just because I've changed my mind about being a murderer, doesn't mean I will betray you. I just can't allow you set the bomb.'

'It's already done and will detonate in less than five minutes!'

'Oh Good God...' The blood drained from his skin. 'We have to stop it!' Releasing her, he began tugging frantically at the neck of the goose, pulling back the flaps of skin.

She seized his arm. 'If you won't think of me or France, think of yourself! They're planning to send you to the Russian front!'

Fiercely, he shook her off. 'But I know how to make things right with the Abwehr. I know the café on the corner of the Rue St Catherine is a hive of the Resistance...'

'You're going to betray them?'

'It's my duty as a German, and the only thing that will convince the Abwehr that I'm innocent of treachery. Don't worry, I'll let you escape before I say anything. I'll tell our guests that you're sick and have gone to lie down and you can slip out. We'll meet again after the war...'

Catriona reached up under her skirt. In one deft move, as she'd been trained, she cocked the pistol with one hand and rammed it hard into his ribs, aiming upwards.

A look of bewildered horror passed over Frederik's face – a second's realisation – as she pulled the trigger, while simultaneously knocking a stack of silver dessert dishes to the floor with her elbow. He sank to his knees, then backwards. As the metal bowls clattered furiously across the ceramic tiles she leant over her lover and – also as she had been taught – shot him again, pushing the muzzle hard into his flesh to deaden the sound. The second-bullet rule was to make sure of death, and also to collapse the nervous system.

As the plates stopped rolling around on the tiles, she carefully opened the door and peeped out. Down the hallway, German voices were deep in discussion. She came back for the platter. She had to step around Frederik as he lay on the tiles, blood pooling beneath him. Feeling like she was made of ice, she repaired the damage to the garnish and walked carefully down the hallway to the dining room.

'I'm so sorry, we had a bit of a catastrophe in the kitchen when a shelf came off the wall. I've asked Frederik to fix it about five times! But anyway, he is just clearing up and he'll be out in just a moment.' Smiling sweetly, she placed the goose in the middle of the table.

'Ah, the *pièce de résistance*,' Otto remarked with a grin. Catriona didn't react to the choice of word. Resistance indeed.

Amazed at how she managed to keep the tremor out of her hands, she poured a glass of claret for each of the Abwehr agents, draining the bottle. 'We need another bottle, gentlemen. Please excuse me.'

She left the dining room, slipped out of the front door and fled on tiptoe downstairs. The main door lock was fiddly and Catriona had to struggle for at least thirty seconds to open it but eventually she managed it. She forced herself to walk, not run away from the building.

She had just reached the corner when the deafening sound of an explosion shook the ground beneath her feet. She'd got out just in time. As she glanced back, the entire front of their building collapsed onto the street – people were screaming, rushing in all directions. She ran with the rest and there, waiting for her just as promised, was the doctor's car. Yves handed her a bag of clothes as she climbed into the back of his car. 'You're alone?'

Catriona was only able to nod. She felt numb.

'Very well then, let's go.' He pulled away from the kerb. Several military vehicles were passing them in the opposite direction, speeding towards the explosion.

Catriona tried as best she could in the confined space to change into a plain grey dress and cardigan he had supplied. She wiped off the elaborately applied makeup using just her spit and a corner of the red dress and shook out her hair before tying it back in a simple bun.

Yves dropped her to the very barn where she had spent her first night. 'Wait down at the back there. Our people are watching this place from all approaches so you are quite safe but still, best not to take any chances. Someone will come for you. *Bonne chance, et merci.*' And he was gone.

Left alone in the barn, Catriona sat on a hay bale in the dark and waited. Grief and horror tugged at the edges of her mind but she pushed the dark emotions away, refusing to allow herself to think about what she'd just done. Instead, she tried to remember song lyrics. Her teachers in Baker

Street had been adamant that this work was as much of a test of mental endurance as physical. For now, she needed to stay focused. This wasn't over yet. Plenty of time for tears afterwards. She looked upwards – pale moonlight was visible through holes in the roof of the barn. The British could only fly by moonlight so that was good. Yet the Germans would be watching the skies like hawks after the explosion. What if the plane couldn't get here to collect her?

She took deep breaths to steady herself, and checked her watch. Almost eleven thirty. Then eleven forty. Each minute felt like an hour. Eventually she heard the sound of bicycle tyres outside. She crouched down behind the hay bales watching the entrance, and only exhaled when she saw the enormous figure of her uncle enter the barn. She jumped up and ran to him, into his waiting arms.

He hugged her back. 'Oh Catriona, my darling girl, well done, well done. Yves told me you are alone?'

'Yes. Frederik changed his mind at the last minute, said he couldn't go through with it. I...I shot him.'

'Good girl.' He held her closer. 'Well done, my darling.' He was clearly unperturbed at the demise of Frederik. In fact, he couldn't keep the delight from his voice as he told her, 'Word is spreading already, how the Resistance has killed twelve high-ranking Nazis.'

'No, but it was only five… I mean, six.' Her heart throbbed, but she pushed the pain back down inside. She had to remember to count Frederik among her enemies now.

Gaston spluttered with laughter. 'No, twelve! This is a propaganda war, so we must exaggerate!'

She smiled weakly. 'Oh, I see…'

Holding her at arm's length, Gaston looked her up and down. 'Good. Those clothes are perfect. Now, the plane will pick you up in an hour. And it can only stay on the ground for a minute or two, so we'll have to be on time. The landing field is two kilometres by road but we are going cross-country, because it's safer. Come, we have to go.'

Leaving the barn, they headed quickly through fields and over gates, at one point even wading through a stream. By the time they reached the appointed big flat field, Catriona was scratched, wet and exhausted. They crouched in the corner of the meadow, waiting.

'Are you sure it will come?' she whispered. 'Just for me?'

He nodded. 'Of course. The British are happy to have you safe home. Anyway, we got lucky with the timing – the plane was coming tonight anyway, dropping something off or picking someone up nearby – exactly what or where, of course we can't be told.' He sighed in frustration. At the same moment, Catriona heard the faintest hum of an engine coming from the west. In the darkness, someone flashed a light. She panicked.

'What's that?'

'It's alright,' he whispered back. 'It's the British, they guide the planes down using bicycle lamps. When the plane lands you run like hell, alright? Mémé and Pépé send you all of their love as do Marie-Clare and Loic. And I know your mother is looking down and her heart is bursting with pride and relief, just like mine.' As the plane came in to land, he embraced her tightly. *'Au revoir ma niece courageuse, à la prochaine.'*

She hugged him back and then ran as fast as she could. A hatch opened in the belly of the plane as it idled on the grass. A strong hand pulled her up into a tiny space; the hatch slammed shut and the pilot clambered back into his cockpit. Within seconds, the plane was bumping across the field; it gained speed and was once again airborne.

In the darkness, Catriona crouched uncomfortably. The noise from the engine was deafening. Her whole body vibrated. She clung to a rope handle as they rose higher and higher. The Lysander had been stripped out inside to make maximum space for people and supplies but it meant she was jammed almost in the tail of the plane. There were wooden crates all around her and to make things even more uncomfortable, another person was wedged between her and the pilot's seat: someone with a coat pulled up over their head, who – incredibly – was fast asleep.

Catriona wriggled around, trying to find a way to sleep herself. Impossible. This journey was going to be interminable. The lighter in her bra stuck into her flesh uncomfortably – but she didn't take it out because she found the feel of it comforting. She had failed to find her father and she had killed the man she'd thought she loved, her only solace was that she carried with her the only object that her father had ever treasured.

CHAPTER 11

'We're in England, Miss! Wakey, wakey!'

Slowly, Catriona opened her eyes. The pilot was leaning over her.

'England? Already? Oh thank God...' She sat up, aching in every bone. She could hardly believe that she'd slept in such an awkward position but tiredness had won out over discomfort. The hatch in the belly of the plane was already open, and the sleeping man was gone, and now the pilot jumped down and stood waiting to help her out. On the tarmac, she stretched and tried to feel her feet.

'Are you alright?' asked the pilot – a young spotty lad, with bright red hair.

'Nothing a hot bath and a long sleep won't solve,' she answered him with a smile. It felt strange to be speaking English again.

'That's the spirit. Ah, here they come.' Two military vehicles were buzzing towards them across the tarmac. 'I'll leave you to talk to the powers that be.' He walked away in the direction of a large hangar.

One of the cars stopped far off in the middle of the

tarmac, to pick up a tall man in a long dark coat who was already walking in the direction of the wooden out-buildings. Her fellow passenger, she assumed. Watching his lanky body as he climbed into the car, she thought for a moment there was something strangely familiar... No. *No.* Stupid wishful thinking. If the man was who she'd briefly imagined he was, he would never have left the plane without even speaking to her.

The other car carried on towards her and stopped, and the uniformed officer who climbed out saluted her. 'Welcome home, Miss!'

* * *

THE FOLLOWING days passed in a blur of debriefing and meetings. Intelligence wanted to know every tiny detail and it seemed it was necessary to repeat it over and over again to many different people. Every time she explained what had happened with Frederik, she had to fight to bury the deep pain in her heart.

At last, her interrogators seemed convinced they knew everything about her mission. She was taken to Baker Street to retrieve her possessions, and then she was on her own.

As she climbed out of the taxi in Holborn, Catriona was relieved to see her house was still standing, and that any windows that had been shattered in her absence had been taped up again by some helpful friend or neighbour. She retrieved her key from the canvas bag she'd left in Baker Street, and let herself in.

On the kitchen table was milk, tea, a loaf and a small packet of butter and a pot of home-made gooseberry jam. Beside it was a card with a stick drawing of two little children on the front.

Delighted, Catriona read:

Grand Père dit que vous retournez aujourd'hui, Catriona. Nous sommes très contents, à bientôt!

Valérie et Olivier.

How sweet it was that they were now referring to Justin as their granddad. She was really looking forward to seeing them too. They were the only 'family' she had left in England; the only ones who loved her. The sound of the key in the door lifted her heart – that must be Elsa now, with the children. Justin must have told her that Catriona was coming home. She hurried into the hall, calling out, *'Bonjour et bienvenue, je suis si heureuse de vous revoir!'*

'And I'm happy to meet you too,' smiled her father, closing the front door behind him. 'But I'd rather speak English if you don't mind.'

For a moment, she could hardly speak any language at all. 'I can't... Oh, God… Oh, oh…' And then she threw herself into his arms, covering his bearded face with kisses. And after that she wept, railing against him for leaving her, for lying to her. 'Where the hell did you get to? Everyone – Gaston, Jean-Claude…' she nearly said 'Frederik', but his name caught in her throat '…everyone was so sure you were dead. You disappeared! Why didn't you let any of us know where you were?'

He stroked her hair, holding her as she cried. 'I'd no choice, pet. Too dangerous. I couldn't send a message to Gaston or to anyone who might send him a message on my behalf, because I couldn't be sure it wouldn't be intercepted and implicate the de Clairands. Karl Fischer seemed to have guessed…'

'That creep!'

He jerked back his head, shocked. 'You met Karl Fischer?'

'Yes.' She felt a fierce stab of satisfaction at having blown Karl to bits. But she didn't want to talk about that for now. Her father clearly didn't know anything about what she'd been up to and she wanted to hear his side of the story first.

'How did you meet him, Catriona? Tell me everything...'

'Don't change the subject. I want to know what happened to you!'

He laughed and shrugged. 'Fine, I'll go first, and then you. But in the meantime, I'm absolutely starving. I don't suppose there's anything to eat in the house?'

Thank goodness for Elsa. 'There is indeed! I can make you tea and a fresh sandwich with homemade gooseberry jam.'

'Oh, you angel!'

'...but only if you keep talking while I do it.'

While she filled the kettle and cut lots of bread and spread it with butter and homemade jam, he sat at the kitchen table and told her everything.

'Well, you know what I was doing in France, clearly. I assume that's why you went tearing off half cocked? So, it seems that Karl Fischer picked up an idea of who I might be from an Oberleutnant called Schroeder, who I was trying to recruit to our side.'

She felt physically sick. How stupid she'd been, to trust Frederik. 'Fre... Oberleutnant Schroeder told Fischer who you were?'

'I don't think he actually *told* him – just let something slip without realising it. He wasn't the sharpest knife in the drawer, Schroeder. Not evil, but weak. Anyway, Fischer definitely wasn't sure of the truth – he was just guessing, feeling his way. He approached me, saying he hated Hitler and could I do something to get him out to London. I didn't trust him and I said I'd no idea what the hell he was on about, and... Well, it all turned a bit nasty. He had me picked up, and I got a right going over from three big thickos he ordered to beat seven bells out of me. They must have smuggled me out of the city while I was still unconscious. Fischer didn't want Schroeder to know what had happened, because he was trying to entrap him.'

Keeping her hand as steady as she could, Catriona set a steaming mug of tea in front of him. 'I met Oberleutnant Schroeder as well, as it happens.'

He was taken aback. 'Good God, Catriona – what have you been up to?'

'He spoke to me about you,' she said, ignoring the question. 'He told me that Fischer told him that you'd got on a train to Paris. Obviously, he was too stupid to realise Fischer was lying.' She tried to keep her voice calm and business-like. She'd hate her father to know that she had developed feelings, not just for a Nazi but for such a weak, pathetic man.

Kieran smiled grimly. 'I did get on a train. A transport train.'

'Oh God.' Even though he was clearly safe, sitting right here in front of her, Catriona's stomach tightened with fear. She sat down at the table, placing the plate piled with bread and jam between them. 'How did you escape?'

'Somewhere up near Poitiers, the train stopped. I don't know what was going on but the soldier supposed to be guarding us was asleep, so myself and a few others broke out of the carriage, and we just ran for it. I managed eventually to make contact with one of the British circuits, and they were happy enough for me to stay on in France, liaising between London and the French on the ground. Of course, I could never show my face around Bordeaux again. So I was knocking around Tours, the Loire, that neck of the woods, and I'd still be there if a fellow called Justin hadn't insisted I be told by London that my daughter was in Bordeaux and soon to be airlifted out. I demanded they get me out at the same time, so I could be sure you were safe...'

She couldn't believe it. 'So it *was* you on the plane! Why didn't you talk to me?'

'Because the deal was, if they brought us both back together, you and I were not to share any information before our debriefing, to preserve the accuracy of our memories. And the easiest way to do that was to pretend to be asleep. I was so happy when you actually fell asleep for real yourself, and I could sit and look at you all the way to England!'

She beamed at him. 'And now you can look at me as much as you like, for the rest of your life!'

He smiled back at her – but instead of answering, he took another bite of his bread and gooseberry jam.

She glared at him suspiciously. 'We *are* going to stay together, aren't we?'

'For a while. But I'm working for the Resistance, Catriona. I have to go back.'

She felt that old painful stab of abandonment. 'You're not going back without me!'

'Yes I am.' He fixed her with a determined stare. 'You haven't told me your story yet, and I'm not even sure I can stand to hear it. But it's clear that you've put yourself in terrible danger by chasing around after me. And you are never, ever, *ever* to do anything as foolish as that ever again, do I make myself clear?'

She said stubbornly, her hands clenched in her lap, 'I wasn't being foolish.'

He sighed and relented. 'Brave, then. But it's a fine line, Catriona, between brave and foolish. I won't say I'm not proud of you, getting the Brits to drop you into France, to find me. And I suspect your mother would be proud of you too – in fact, I know she would: she was as brave as a lion herself. But she's not here to mind you and you're all I've got. So here you stay, and if everything goes wrong and the Germans invade, you're to get yourself to Ireland no matter what. DeValera will resist joining the British with his last breath, no matter what Churchill threatens, so Ireland's neutrality should hold.'

She sat in silence.

Her father lit a cigarette with a box of matches from his pocket. He exhaled and then spoke again slowly: 'Listen, darling. I swore to Eloise's memory that I'd look after you…'

'Where's your silver lighter?' she interrupted.

His face darkened. 'Gone. Those thugs stole it. The last thing I had of your mother. Of my darling Eloise…' Just saying his wife's name caused a catch in his voice. And then he realised that his daughter was smiling at him. He stared at her, bemused. 'What?'

She didn't answer but jumped up and ran out into the hallway to find the canvas bag and dug her hand into the side pocket. She returned to the kitchen and placed the flat of her hand on the table in front of him, then lifted it to reveal the lighter.

'*What?* How? Where… *How* did you get this?' In joy and shock, he grabbed his precious lighter and kissed it before reading the inscription over and over again. 'Where did you find this, Catriona? What were you really doing in France? Tell me!'

So she told him the whole story. How she *had* been trying to find him, but how she had also been fighting for the cause, the same as Kieran. And how she nearly got sick when she saw Fischer with his lighter, and how she'd managed to steal it before killing six Nazis (or twelve, if you believed Gaston). She didn't admit to her feelings for Frederik. That was all in the past now, because it had to be. And Kieran, if he suspected, didn't press her on it. He just got to his feet and drew Catriona into a hug and whispered 'Thank God you're safe. You're your mother's daughter, Catriona, and I'm so proud of you. I love you my darling girl, I love you.'

THE END

I sincerely hope you enjoyed this novella and if you did you might consider leaving me a review.

To download a free book and to read more Jean Grainger fiction, or sign up for her newsletter, go to her website www.jeangrainger.com

If you would like to read another of my books, please read on for a preview of my bestselling WW2 novel, So Much Owed.

So Much Owed

Prologue

12th December 1918

*F*rom the outside, it was barely recognisable. Gaping holes in the walls and piles of smoking rubble had irrevocably altered the once imposing facade of *l'Hôpital Saint Germain*. The Allied propaganda machine had claimed the Battle of Amiens as a great victory – a turning point, spelling an end to the horrific futility of trench warfare. It was here in Amiens, the victors crowed, that the Germans had stumbled their first steps towards surrender. Yet as Dr Richard Buckley picked his way through the decimated city, he saw nothing about Amiens to suggest a city basking in the glory of victory. Instead, he found himself thinking: *So this is what winning looks like.*

He climbed what was left of the marble steps leading to the ornate entrance. Everything was so different from when he was last here four months ago. Gone was the officious Reverend Mother, who had vetted all entrants to the hospital with her suspicious eye. Gone too, the all-pervasive smell of beeswax and disinfectant that had permeated the quiet, ordered corridors of the past. Now the smell reminded him of Willy McCarthy's butcher shop in Skibbereen, where he and his school friends had gone one day to see the farmyard animals being slaughtered. The sickly scent of their dying had haunted him for years. Now the same mingled odour of blood, flesh, bone and fear again assailed his nostrils. It no longer made him physically sick – one can get used to anything, it seemed – yet as he strode through the foyer and up the stairs, he found it a struggle to endure the anguished cries of the wounded all around him. Two years spent treating the casualties of war had done nothing to desensitise him to the suffering of others.

'*Excusez-moi.*' He tried to seize the attention of a passing nun. Like everyone else here, she looked exhausted; her once-white uniform was spattered with bloodstains, some brown with age. '*Vous connaissez Solange Allingham…*'

'*Non, Monsieur.*' She shook off his arm and hurried on.

He had been moved further up the line last August, to where his services were in even greater demand. It seemed the turnover of hospital staff in his absence had been so rapid that there was no one left here who knew him. Perhaps he should have worn his uniform, but he had taken it off the day the armistice was declared and had vowed never to put it on again. He wanted nothing to do with the sense of triumph expounded by the top brass. Not because he was Irish and, therefore, it was not his country's glory, but because he was sickened by the whole bloody thing. He'd endured their congratulations at his decision to do the right thing, despite his nationality, with gritted teeth. It was pointless trying to explain his motivation had nothing to do with patriotism or a desire to defeat anyone, and everything to do with trying to alleviate suffering. Anyway, those men who aired such views were usually patients, and so he treated them as best he could and avoided any discussions on the subject.

HE TRIED AGAIN, THIS time approaching a young nurse with red hair who just might be Irish.

'Excuse me – do you know Madame Solange Allingham?'

She stared at him as if amazed to see a fully intact man and answered him in a west of Ireland accent, 'Yes, she's in the theatre, but I think she's due a break sometime soon. Whether or not she'll get it is another thing. We've both been on duty,' she glanced at the watch pinned to the front of her uniform, 'twenty-nine hours now. If you want to wait, she'll come out this way. *If* she comes out. Now, please excuse me. If I don't lie down, I'll fall down.'

Richard sat on a wooden bench and leaned his tall frame against the dark-brown wainscoting. He also was exhausted. He thought he should probably go to a ward, offer to help, but he simply couldn't. He'd worked more or less constantly for two years, only going home on leave twice during that time, and apart from those brief visits, never taking a day off. He had treated the wounded day and night and only stopped when he felt his exhaustion was a danger to the patients. He would then sleep dreamlessly for a few hours and begin the whole bloody process again. The waves of battered and broken young men in front of him, many of them begging to die, never subsided. Some survived, a great many more didn't, and thousands were left with injuries so horrific that perhaps death would have been preferable to life.

His tiredness was playing tricks on his mind. Every time a doctor came round the corner, he found himself thinking it was Jeremy. Even though he had seen so many young men die, Richard still found it hard to accept that his best friend had joined the rest. He had been so vital, so much larger than life – smiling and joking and keeping everyone's spirits up. Yet it had turned out he was mortal like everyone else; apparently, he'd been killed in a bomb blast on his way to the hospital after a much-needed sleep. Even the nurse who had written to him with the news, herself so used to sudden death, had sounded shocked. Such a beloved doctor gone and so close to the end too – another week and it would have been all over.

Now Richard had nothing left to do but to collect Solange and bring her home with him. Jeremy should have been the one to take care of her after the war, but that was not to be. Solange Allingham had no one else to protect her now – her parents were dead, her brothers both killed at Verdun. Jeremy and Richard had talked about this – if either of them was killed. Somehow, Richard had assumed that if either of them died, it would be him. He was so dull and uninteresting, compared to his friend. Yet in the end, it had been the lively, ever-smiling Jeremy who had died. And now it was down to Richard to take care of his best friend's sad, young widow.

CHAPTER 1

20th January 1919

Solange Allingham gazed out the window of the black Morris Oxford at the sodden fields. The endless journey through England by train and the choppy crossing to Ireland had barely registered with her. She could feel nothing except a dragging despair, deep within her. Even the rhythmic slosh of the car's wipers seemed to beat out the mantra, 'Jeremy is dead, Jeremy is dead.' They had been planning to buy a vineyard in the Dordogne after the war; they were going to have a huge family – three boys, three girls. *'Jeremy is dead, Jeremy is dead.'*

Gradually, the green rolling hills of the southeastern counties of Wexford and Waterford gave way to rugged stone-filled fields. She kept on catching distant glimpses of a grey, cold ocean. Beside her, Richard drove in silence, his vivid green eyes focused on the wet road ahead, his sandy hair neatly cut and combed. How he and Jeremy had been such good friends amazed her. Her Jeremy had always been so bright and funny and full of life. This quiet, shy Irish doctor entirely lacked that sort of charm. When he spoke, it was always slow and deliberate. He was painstakingly methodical in his work, irrespective of any chaos that surrounded him. Yet she had seen injured soldiers stop screaming in agony when Dr Buckley spoke to them or touched them. 'The gentle giant,' Jeremy had dubbed him, and he was indeed big – well over six feet tall, with a deep voice she knew his patients found reassuring.

'Not long now. We'll be in Skibbereen by six, I should think. I hope you aren't too uncomfortable?' His eyes never left the road.

'No, thank you.' She hesitated, seeking the English words. Her mind felt like it was wrapped in wet cotton wool, and all she really wanted to do was sleep. 'I am fine.' In the weeks since Jeremy had died, she had barely spoken, in either her native French or her husband's English. Not that she had learnt much English from Jeremy – he had always said he was too romantic and passionate to be

Anglo-Saxon and so spoke in French to her most of the time.

All the nurses had been in love with the young doctor with his thick, wavy hair and warm hazel eyes; he had flirted outrageously with all of them, but they knew there was nothing in it – he only had eyes for Solange Galliard. He had pursued her relentlessly from when he was first assigned to the hospital, ignoring her protests that she was engaged to Armand De La Croix, the son of a local banker. Jeremy saw this as no obstacle whatsoever: she simply had to break off the engagement and marry him instead. It was impossible to do anything else, he'd claimed – she had bewitched him with her deep azure eyes and her black corkscrew curls, forever threatening to liberate themselves from the starched white veil of her nurse's uniform. He told her regularly that she occupied his every thought, waking and sleeping, and, despite herself, she had fallen in love with the incorrigible English doctor. When he talked, he made her laugh till tears flowed down her cheeks, and when he touched her, she tingled with desire. She had married him and was the happiest girl on earth.

Back in 1914, the war had been seen as something to be over by Christmas. The girls had giggled with delight at the vast numbers of handsome soldiers arriving daily. It had all seemed so romantic, the men so gallant – a bit of a lark really, as Jeremy termed it. How wrong they all were. The fun and high spirits of those early days had quickly given way to scenes of unprecedented human misery. Those scenes would haunt all those who witnessed them for the rest of their lives.

Solange wondered if Jeremy would even recognise her if he were to see her now. Grief had taken its toll on the curvaceous body he had loved; her once round cheeks were hollow, and dark shadows circled her blue eyes. At twenty-six, her jet-black hair had become suddenly threaded with silver hairs. The person she had been before the war seemed a distant stranger to her now. She suspected the carefree girl of her youth had died along with that whole generation of young men. All gone now, and Jeremy gone with them.

'There is a rug on the back seat if you're cold.' Richard's voice interrupted her reverie.

'No, thank you. I am fine.' She realised her answer was a repetition of her response to his earlier enquiry so she added, with an attempt at enthusiasm, 'Ireland is a very pretty country. Quite like Brittany in places, I think.' She knew her voice sounded flat and colourless. She couldn't help it.

He nodded thoughtfully. 'Yes, I'm glad you like it. Though, of course, when the sun shines, it's much better. When we were students in England, Jeremy often came here on holidays. He complained that it never stopped raining. I tried to get him to consider moving here after the war, but he said he would rather get a suntan in France than rust in Ireland any day.'

They both smiled at the memory of him; his presence was almost tangible between them in the car.

'Thank you for doing this for me,' Solange began again. 'You have been so kind. I cannot imagine how it would have been if I would have stayed in France. I don't know if I can survive now, but at least here has no memories. I will try to be of service to you and your family.'

Richard drove and sighed deeply as if weighing up how best to phrase what he was going to say next.

'Solange, I'm not bringing you to Dunderrig to be of service to us, I am bringing you to be a member of our family. Please understand that. It's your home for as long as you want it to be. We, Edith and I, don't expect anything from you, but I, we, both hope that coming here will help you. I can't imagine how hard it must be, considering all you have lost. Not just Jeremy, but your parents, your brothers. It's almost too much to bear. We just want to help, in any way that we can. Jeremy would have taken care of Edith had the situation been reversed. We talked about it, you know. What we would do if either one of us didn't make it. I know if it had been me who was killed then you and Jeremy would have helped Edith. So please, you are family as far as we are concerned. You don't owe us a thing.'

In the four years she had known Richard Buckley, this was the longest speech she had ever heard him make. His voice was cracking with emotion and it was clear his offer came from the heart. She hardly knew what to say – she sat in silent gratitude as he drove the narrow, twisty road.

'Down there is Skibbereen, but this is where we turn off,' he said, taking a slow right at a signpost marked 'Dunderrig'. 'I wrote to Edith to let her know we were arriving this evening, so she will be expecting us. Though naturally, she has been very tired of late.'

'Of course. She has only a few more weeks to go?' Solange enquired politely.

'Two weeks, perhaps. No more than three. I would have given anything to have been here to help her. She has suffered badly with sickness throughout this pregnancy. And she had to cope with the loss of my mother and father too, within a few days of each other. Thank God the influenza spared my wife, if not my poor parents. She has had so much to cope with.'

'It will feel strange for you to be home and not to see them. Even as an adult, you are never ready to lose your parents.' She was conscious that her voice had grown heavy with her own pain and made an effort to be stronger for him. 'But you must be very excited to see your wife after all this time.'

'Yes, I am.' A brief smile but nothing more.

She glanced at him, questioningly. Richard very rarely mentioned Edith; Solange had often speculated with Jeremy about what kind of marriage the Buckleys had – practical, passionate, romantic? When she wondered what Mrs Buckley was like, Jeremy told her that he had met Edith only briefly and explained how he had dragged his shy best friend to a dance while they were still at medical college in England. To his surprise, Richard spent his evening talking about Ireland with a cool but beautiful blonde from Dublin. Only weeks later they qualified, and Jeremy signed up for France and met Solange while Richard went to work as a doctor in Ireland and ended up marrying the Dublin girl. Solange's only knowledge of Edith was based on the photo Richard had of her on his desk in the hospital; it showed a tall and elegant woman, beautifully dressed. She also knew that Richard had seen his wife very briefly eight months before, when in Dublin on leave – a leave that had been cut short before he'd been able to travel home to Cork to visit his parents, then still alive and well. Poor Richard. 'And are you also excited to become a Papa?'

'Yes. I am.' The same answer, but this time the smile was warmer.

THE HOUSE WAS SET back from the road and was impressive in its size and architecture. While not a *château* by any standard, it still seemed to be a very large house for a couple to inhabit alone. It was built of a buttery stone with limestone edging, and despite its grand size appeared welcoming, with lights blazing in each window, promising a warm and inviting end to her long, tiring journey. The tree-lined avenue passed through gardens that were beautifully kept, even during their winter sleep. Large sections of the housefront were covered with crimson-and-gold creeping ivy and as they drew level with the large, bottle-green front door – the car's wheels crunching on the gravel – Solange admired the blood-red Poinsettia spilling from pots in wild profusion on either side of the door. Perhaps Edith was a keen gardener. She hoped so because she loved gardens too – it would give them something to talk about.

Richard opened the car door and offered her his arm to assist her out. Standing, she found she was stiff and sore, and suddenly longed for a bath and a good night's sleep. As he opened the front door, a plump, matronly woman with iron-grey hair and a currant-bun face came hurrying from the back section of the house.

'Dr Richard, you're home! You're as welcome as the flowers of May. Let me have a look at you! God in heaven, you're skin and bone! We'll have to feed you up. Oh, 'tis wonderful to have you home, so it is. I can't believe 'tis two years since you set foot in Dunderrig. Wouldn't your mother and father be just delighted to see you, God rest them home safe and sound. They never stopped worrying about you, God be good to them.' Tears filled the woman's eyes.

Solange stood by as Richard put his arms around the grey-haired woman and held her tightly.

'You were so good to them, Mrs Canty. My mother's last letter told how much ye did to ease my poor father's passing, and how skilful ye were at nursing her. I can't believe she won't be in the kitchen or he in his surgery ever again.'

He spoke quietly; their loss was shared. Mrs Canty was clearly much more than a housekeeper – more like one of the family. After a few minutes, he stepped back and indicated Solange.

'Mrs Canty, this is Madame Solange Allingham, Jeremy's wife.'

The woman hurried towards Solange, dabbing her eyes with the corner of her apron.

'I beg your pardon, I didn't see you there. What must you think of us at all? You are very welcome to Dunderrig, pet, and I'm sorry it's only me here to greet ye. We didn't know exactly when to expect you, you see. My Eddie is out and about somewhere, and Mrs Buckley is upstairs having a lie-down. She's been very out of sorts all day.'

She took Solange's hand while sadly shaking her head.

'I remember your husband well – a lovely lad and no mistake. He was like a ray of sunshine around the place when he used to visit. Dr Richard's mother, God rest her soul, used to knock a great kick out of him altogether – the antics and tricks acting out of him! I was so sorry to hear he had been killed, and ye only a young couple starting out in your lives. 'Twas a terrible thing that war. So many grand lads like Jeremy, gone forever.'

The woman spoke so quickly that Solange struggled to understand her – but she could tell enough to be moved by the kind way this woman spoke about her dead husband and warmed to her at once.

'Thank you, Mrs Canty. Yes, my husband often spoke about the happy times he enjoyed in Ireland.' Solange hoped her English was clear enough.

Whether Mrs Canty fully understood her or not, she seemed satisfied with Solange's halting answer. 'You're very welcome here, especially now. God knows, with the new baby arriving any minute, we'll be all up in the air soon. I'll tell you, Dr Richard, she's not great at all today. I've been trying to get her to eat a bit all day long, but she's not having a bar of it. You'd think she'd be all excitement over having you home after all this time! Normally, women get a bit of a boost just before, you know, getting things ready for the baby and all that, but she just lies in bed, the only thing she's interested in is writing letters...'

'Thank you, Mrs Canty, that will be all.'

Both Richard and Mrs Canty turned with a start, and

Solange followed their eyes to the top of the stairs from where the cold, sharp voice had come.

'It is perhaps not so inconceivable that I would not wish to eat, given the standard of cuisine in this house. Please attend to your duties.'

The haughty tone brooked no argument. A tall, blonde woman was descending the staircase, which curved elegantly around the walls into the large square entrance hall. She was dressed in an ivory silk gown, over which she wore a contrasting coffee-coloured robe, and she moved remarkably gracefully, given the advanced stage of her pregnancy; despite the large bump, she was slender, almost thin. She looked pale and tired, but also something else. She seemed to exude disdain, not just for the verbose Mrs Canty but for her entire surroundings. She certainly seemed to show no delight at the safe return of her husband.

'Edith, you look wonderful, blooming. Mrs Canty was telling us you haven't been well? It's so good to see you.' Richard crossed to the bottom of the stairs, offering his hand to assist her down the last few steps. She allowed him to take it and turned a powdered cheek for him to kiss, but Solange could see her actions lacked enthusiasm. Richard must have noticed it too – having pecked his wife lightly, he released her limp fingers and retreated a few steps, looking around him, clearly searching for something else to say. His eyes alighted on Solange. 'Edith, this is Solange Allingham, Jeremy's wife.'

Edith Buckley heaved a huge, sarcastic sigh as she approached Solange. 'Yes, Richard, I did gather who this was. You wrote to me several times to tell me she was coming, and it is not as if Dunderrig is such a hive of social activity that I would confuse the guests. Mrs Allingham, what on earth possessed you to leave France for this godforsaken place?'

Uncertain how to respond, Solange silently extended her own hand, but Edith ignored it.

'Oh well, you're here now, so you will have to make the best of it. Presumably, you will either expire from boredom or food poisoning, but if you are determined to take your chances... Oh, Mrs Canty, are you still here?'

Mrs Canty marched off furiously to the kitchen, saying loudly how someone had to prepare a 'good, wholesome meal' for the poor travellers. Richard seemed unsure what he should do next. He made to put his hand on his wife's back but the look she gave him was so frosty, he changed his mind.

Solange hurried to lighten the mood. 'Madame Buckley, I must thank you for inviting me into your home. Please believe me, after the past few years in France, a quiet life is something I wholeheartedly desire, so do not be concerned I will be bored. Besides, when the new little one arrives, it will be a very busy household. I hope to be of some service.' She tried to infuse her voice with gratitude and friendliness to bring some much-needed warmth into the situation.

Edith shrugged. 'I suppose so. But I warn you, it will all seem deathly dull. I am sorry about your husband. Still, if countries insist on colonising smaller nations then war must be an inevitable outcome.'

Solange was nonplussed. Was Edith saying that Jeremy deserved to die because of the past decisions of English and French rulers? Surely she could not be so callous. She glanced at Richard, who had coloured with embarrassment.

Nonchalantly changing the subject, Edith addressed her husband, 'Richard, please contact Dr Bateman to come out. I'm not feeling well, and I need to consult him. I'm going back to bed. Welcome home. Please don't disturb me until he arrives.' She turned away.

Richard followed his wife across the hall to the foot of the sweeping stairs. 'Perhaps it's something I can help you with? It is rather a long way for Bateman to come…'

'Richard,' Edith said wearily, without looking back at him. 'While I accept you are a doctor, you are not *my* doctor. You have been conspicuous by your absence throughout my confinement so it would be wholly inappropriate for you to involve yourself in my care at this late stage. Please contact Dr Bateman as soon as possible.' Moving wearily but not slowly, she climbed the stairs.

'Very well. If that's what you want, then of course I'll contact him – and then maybe we could have tea?'

Richard was almost pleading. But Edith had already disappeared into a room on the second floor, and his request was met with the closing of the door behind her. He turned anxiously to Solange.

'She is very tired. And she is so devoted to the cause of Irish independence. She didn't mean anything against poor Jeremy. Her opinions…she is not a supporter of the Allies. But of course, she doesn't support the other side either. I'm afraid I have to leave you a moment to call Dr Bateman. Can you take a seat here, until Mrs Canty returns? She will see you to your room and feed you to within an inch of your life and hopefully you'll start to feel normal again.' Then he backtracked as if worrying that he had sounded as crass as his wife. 'I mean obviously not normal, not after everything, but maybe you can feel just a little better. Welcome to Dunderrig.'

While Solange waited for the housekeeper's re-emergence, she studied her new surroundings. The entrance hall was warm and welcoming, in stark contrast to its mistress. It was as generously proportioned as any reception room and carpeted with a rich-red-and-gold rug. The furniture – a hall stand, a writing table and chair, a loudly ticking grandfather clock, and the upholstered chaise longue on which she had seated herself – were all highly polished. Oil paintings – landscapes and horses, mainly – adorned the silk-covered walls. The cantilevered staircase had a deep pile runner at its centre. A passageway led from the hall towards the back of the house. It was down this that Mrs Canty had disappeared and, based on the aromas of baking, it was connected to the kitchen. To her left and right were four large oak doors, also richly polished and all closed. Richard had gone through one of them into what was clearly a doctor's surgery. Why had Edith insisted Richard call her a different doctor? If she, Solange, had been pregnant with Jeremy's child, her husband would have been the only doctor she would have trusted to attend her.

She glanced up to the second floor. The mahogany banister became a small but ornate balcony for the rooms above, all the doors of which opened out onto the landing. The effect meant the entranceway felt like a stage and the upper gallery the viewing point. Solange felt exposed and wished that Mrs Canty would reappear. She dreaded the possibility of Edith's return.

'Ah Lord, did he leave you here all on your own? Where's he gone to, in the name of God? I don't know what's happening to everyone in this house, honest to God, I don't. God knows, in the mistress's time, Mrs Buckley now, I mean old Mrs Buckley, Dr Richard's mother, no visitor would have been left alone in the hall, but I don't know, things are very different around here these days. Poor Dr Richard, home after that terrible war and you'd think his wife would be happy to see him anyway.'

The housekeeper's voice dropped to a whisper as she pointed theatrically upwards while ushering Solange down the passageway into the kitchen.

'She's a bit of a handful, and she can be very cutting when she wants to be. Poor old Dr Buckley and the mistress, God be good to them, nearly drove themselves cracked trying to please her, but the day young Dr Richard left her here in Dunderrig while he went off to the war was a sad day for this house. At first, he'd taken work in Dublin to please her, but he couldn't rest easy when he heard from your husband about all the terrible goings-on at the front, and in the end, nothing would satisfy him but to follow Jeremy to France. He thought his wife would understand how she would be better off waiting for him in Dunderrig, and maybe look after his parents for him. But she stayed above in her room with a face that'd turn milk sour. Sure, even when the poor doctor got the flu earlier this year and we lost him, and the mistress less than a week later, not a budge out of herself above! And there were never two kinder people, God rest them. They were lovely, lovely people. I know she's from Dublin and not used to life in the country, but she's stuck in something to do with the rising and all that nonsense. Her father was some kind of a bigwig professor in the college up there, and he knew them all, Pearse and Yeats and all of them. We're not fancy enough at all for her, to my way of thinking. Sure, she just writes letters all day and gets letters back, too. I don't know who they're from, but 'tisn't right for a married woman to be going on with that kind of thing. Though I keep my own counsel, because of course, Dr Richard won't hear a word against her. He was forever writing to us to make sure she was all right and what have you, and Mrs Buckley decided he had enough to worry about over there so she told him 'twas all grand, but I'd say he got a bit of a land when he met her above in Dublin. Though she came back expecting, so I suppose they must have worked it out some kind of a way.' She softened, and chuckled.

Solange found herself standing in the middle of a warm, cosy kitchen that looked out onto a cobbled courtyard. The stones shone in the wet twilight of a winter's day.

'Now, you poor misfortune, you must be perished alive after sitting in that car for so long. My husband Eddie – he does the gardens, you see, and a bit of fetching and carrying around the house – he drove it down to the boat yesterday and got the train and bus back so 'twould be there for ye when ye got off the boat, and he said it was cosier on the train by far. Sit down there, let you, and I'll get you a bowl of soup to warm your bones. Were you ever here in Ireland before?'

Mrs Canty's patter was so like a babbling brook – comforting and restful, whatever its content – it took Solange a second to realise she had been asked a question.

'In Ireland? *Jamais*... I mean, no, never. Jeremy always said he would bring me here when the war was over but... Well, that was not meant to be.' Solange tried to recover, but Mrs Canty noticed the break in her voice. Turning from the large range, she crossed the floor and took Solange by surprise by enveloping her in a warm hug.

'Your husband was a grand lad entirely, and I'm sure you brought him great joy in his short life. 'Tis better you had him, even for a short time, and had the happiness of a good marriage than years stretching out without it.' And she nodded knowingly again in the direction of upstairs.

Anxious not to take sides, Solange said, 'Perhaps things will be better after the arrival of the new baby. Madame Buckley is probably just tired. I do not know myself as I have no children, but I imagine the last weeks can be exhausting. So, perhaps, once the baby is born safe and well, Madame Buckley will feel better.'

'Hmm. I don't know about that. I was never blessed with children either, but I know plenty of mothers and none of them are like herself above, I can tell you that.'

Mrs Canty placed a steaming hot bowl of creamy vegetable soup and a slice of brown soda bread thickly spread with butter on the table in front of Solange. After the deprivation in France, the richness of the food was glorious. Realising that she was very hungry, she ate greedily while Mrs Canty continued in the same vein.

'I don't know what to make of her. She arrived here with all her grand notions, but then she didn't change one thing about the place. I mean, even before she was expecting, you'd think a young bride coming into a place, especially a place like Dunderrig, would want to put her own stamp on the house. But 'twas as if she was a guest, and one that mightn't be staying at that. Very vexed she was with Dr Richard, over him joining up, I suppose, but 'twasn't as if she was heart-broken without him. Sure, she has no *meas* on him at all; she treats him no better than an auld stray dog. His parents now, the old doctor and Mrs Buckley, they idolised young Richard. He was their only one, you see. They nearly went out of their minds with worry when he went over there to France, and who could blame them? Sure, what has France to do with us here?'

Suddenly, remembering that Solange was French, Mrs Canty corrected herself hastily, 'Not that we thought the other side should win or anything… But it's just they were so worried, and him the only son of the house and all, but when they heard he was going to be with Jeremy, well that made them feel a bit easier in their minds. They were mad about Jeremy. We all were.'

'My husband loved you all, too. And he never wanted Richard to leave his parents. In truth, he was angry when Richard followed him. He didn't want his friend to be in danger, even though when Richard came, Jeremy was so happy to see him and so glad to have the help of such a good doctor.'

Remembering her young husband's concern for his friend, Solange felt very far from home, and from him.

Jeremy had been the essential link between her and Richard; in Amiens, she had only ever met the Irish doctor in Jeremy's company. Richard had never called on her separately or even chatted to her apart from a polite enquiry after her health. Yet here she was in Richard Buckley's house, in this foreign country so far from anything she'd ever known, and without Jeremy. Perhaps this had been a terrible mistake. Yet there was nothing left to which to return. *Maman and Papa both gone, Pierre and Jean-Paul too, and the city in ruins. You can't ever go back, only forward.* She had no choice. Richard had saved her from a life inhabited only by ghosts. At least, here in this strange place, she could be of use – help with the new baby, and begin again. Richard had thrown her a lifeline, and though at the moment drowning seemed like a more appealing option, she knew that she could and would survive.

'NOW PETEEN, WE BETTER get you to bed,' announced Mrs Canty as she ushered Solange upstairs and into a pretty room overlooking the garden. The walls were covered with an exotic bird of paradise wallpaper, in royal blue and gold, and on the teak double bed lay a beautifully embroidered cream bedspread. There were a large matching armoire and chest of drawers and a full-length mirror stood on a stand. The room was pleasantly warm and scented by a bunch of snowdrops arranged in a cut-glass bowl on the dresser. Her bags had been delivered to the room, presumably by the reticent Eddie, whom she still hadn't met.

'*Les fleurs*... The flowers. They are beautiful.'

'Oh that's himself, my Eddie, he grows them. Winter and summer he has flowers growing. He has Latin names for everything; you'd be demented trying to remember them all. There's nothing he can't grow, that husband of mine.' Her voice glowed with pride. 'Now so, let you have a good sleep, and we'll see you tomorrow sometime. Don't be in any rush to get up now, do you hear me?'

Solange slept fitfully, despite the comfortable bed. She tossed and turned and dreamed of France, and of her parents – though never of Jeremy. That often struck her as strange, how his loss was like a large gaping hole of pain in her every waking moment, yet once she slept, he never entered her dreams. The countryside was so quiet; only the crowing of a rooster in the early hours disturbed the peace. Lying awake, she decided to make the best of this situation. She would do her utmost to be a good friend to Richard's wife. Though Mrs Canty seemed a kind person, there was probably not a woman on earth whom the housekeeper would have thought good enough for her precious young master. And although Edith had seemed very cold and even rude to her at first, Solange acknowledged that if Jeremy had brought a young widow into their home, she too would have been cautious at first, however much she trusted her husband.

As dawn crept across the sky, she dozed off into a light sleep. She was disturbed by a piercing shriek from across the hall. Dashing out of bed, she threw on her dressing gown and ran in the direction of the sound. She found herself at the door of Edith's bedroom and hesitated, unsure if Edith was in there alone or if Richard had already joined her. A second later, another loud scream rent the air. This time, tentatively, Solange opened the door. The room was in complete darkness; she moved in the direction of the bed.

'Madame Buckley? Are you well?' The words sounded foolish to her ears, but she didn't know what else to say. Moving towards the curtains, she pulled them half open, allowing in sufficient dawn light to see Richard's wife alone in bed, a terrified expression on her face.

'Something… something is happening,' Edith gasped.

Solange ran to the bed and, gently moving back the

covers, discovered Edith's water had broken. Her nightgown was soaking, as was the sheet and presumably the mattress beneath. Despite the pain, Edith was clearly mortified by the mess and was trying to cover it with her hands.

'Please, do not worry, Madame,' Solange said soothingly. 'This is normal. Your baby is now coming. Please stay calm, and I will send for your husband…'

'No!' Edith screamed.

Solange was unsure if the woman's cry related to Richard or to the pain, but Edith was holding her hand so tightly, it would have been impossible for her to move away from the bed anyway.

'No,' repeated Edith, this time as a hiss. 'Not Richard. I don't want him seeing me like this. Not Canty either. Get Dr Bateman back.'

'But Madame, I think there may be no time to send for him. I'm sure your husband will be here any moment.'

Where was he? No one could sleep through these screams. Solange took a deep breath; she must stay calm.

'If you will permit me to examine you, I think we will find that the baby is almost here. Please do not worry, everything is going to be fine.' Solange was trying to measure the time in between the waves of pain that seemed to grip Edith with such savagery. She'd been present at many deliveries and could tell that this labour was very advanced. Had Edith been having contractions for hours and said nothing until she could bear the pain no longer? Was she that resistant to her husband's presence?

'Please Madame, please try to relax. I know it is difficult but please trust me, it will hurt less if you –' Frustratingly, the English would not come to her. 'Breathe slow and deeply,' she finished, relieved to have recalled the words. 'If you can try to relax, you are doing so well, and then the baby will be here very soon, and all of this will be over, I promise.'

Edith's response was another high-pitched scream. Mrs Canty appeared at the door, in her night-robe and bonnet. 'Oh Lord above! It's time, is it? Dr Richard's gone out on a sick call, tonight of all nights, and he only in the door. I don't even know where he is. What should we do?' Mrs Canty's voice was rising to a crescendo of panic.

'Please, don't worry, everything is perfectly normal. I have delivered many babies before.' A white lie – she'd only ever played a supporting role, and that was when she was still in training – but she had to calm the old housekeeper down. 'So Mrs Canty, if you can just help me by… No, there is no point now trying to get towels under her. I think the baby is coming soon. Please, go and wash your hands and sterilise some scissors in boiling water and bring them back to me. Now, Madame, please just breathe, *oui*, yes, very good, you are doing everything beautifully and very soon you will hold your baby in your arms.'

Edith's breathing became deeper and more even as she locked eyes with Solange. Then she screamed again.

'Now, Madame.' Solange attempted to infuse her voice with both kindness and authority. 'The next time you feel the pain, you must push down very hard. Your baby is almost here. Just a few more minutes and all this will be over, everything will be well. Just keep your energy for delivering your baby. You are doing very well.'

It seemed that Edith was beginning to trust her. As the next contraction came, she gripped Solange's hand tightly and pushed with every ounce of strength she had.

'Now Madame, the next one will be the one to deliver your baby. Try to pant, like this…' Solange demonstrated and Edith followed her instructions. The next contraction began to build. Solange moved to the foot of the bed. Between Edith's legs, the head of the baby was crowning.

'Now, just push very hard, and the little one will be here.'

The infant came slipping from Edith's body into Solange's arms. 'Oh, Madame, a little girl, a beautiful little girl!'

She cut the umbilical cord with the scissors and handed the wailing child to a tearful Mrs Canty, who wrapped the tiny body in freshly warmed blankets. Minutes passed as Solange waited for the placenta to follow. Surprisingly, Edith's contractions continued. The pain should have ceased with the delivery of the child, but she seemed to be still in full labour.

'What's happening?' Edith gasped, terror in her eyes. 'Why is it not over? You said it would be over once it was born!'

Solange fought the urge to panic; she looked again between Edith's legs and was astonished to see another head crowning. 'Madame, please do not worry, but there is... Yes, there is another baby. Please, you must push once more.'

With a loud cry from Edith, the second infant slipped out quickly and easily and was also deposited into the waiting arms of Mrs Canty.

'A little boy! Oh, Madame, how wonderful for you!'

The two placentas followed, and finally, Edith lay back on the pillows, exhausted. Solange helped her into a more comfortable position, murmuring soft, soothing words in French. Then she changed the sodden sheets and replaced Edith's nightgown with a fresh one. Throughout this process, the new mother avoided her eyes as if acutely embarrassed by what had just happened. She appeared self-conscious of her body, even in front of the woman who had just assisted her giving birth.

Mrs Canty was busy wrapping up the babies and cooing over them. 'Oh holy mother of God. Oh, missus, ye have a pair of beauties here and no mistake.' She was wiping away tears as the lusty wails of the newborns filled the air. Solange took them from her, wrapped in their warm blankets, and brought them to the head of the bed, preparing to place them in their mother's arms.

'*Félicitations,* congratulations, Madame, they are beautiful. I am sure you and your husband will be very proud of them.'

Edith looked down at her two babies and to Solange's dismay, turned with difficulty onto her side, away from them.

'Please take them away, I need to sleep now.'

'*Oui,* Madame, of course, but perhaps you should feed them first? Then I can take them and bathe them?' Solange suggested.

'No, I shan't be feeding them. Please attend to them and do not disturb me.'

'But Madame, how will I...'

'Canty knows where everything is.' Edith settled down to sleep.

'I wasn't sure she'd go through with it,' Mrs Canty whispered as she and Solange were wrapping up the infants once more, having put napkins on them. 'But by God, it seems she is. She had some bottles and tins sent over from England a few weeks ago. Nestlé, it says on the labels. She told me that's what the baby – well, I suppose it's the babies now – anyway that's what we're to feed them. Not nursing her own babies, did you ever hear the like...'

'Please, just leave.' Edith's voice had regained some of its lost strength.

AN HOUR LATER, AS Solange sat dozing in the rocking chair with both babies asleep in the smart new bassinet beside her, Richard burst into the kitchen. 'Oh Solange, thank God you were here. Eddie only just found me! I was up the mountain at Coakley's farm. I should have left a note, but I thought there was still weeks to go... I'm so sorry you had to manage on your own but thank God you were here. So where is he? Or she?'

The news that there was not one baby but two filled Richard with joy. She had never seen this quiet man so animated and excited. She thought of Jeremy and how he would have loved the children they would never have. So often in bed they had discussed names for their children. She, favouring English names to match their surname, he arguing for French. He had loved France and everything about it. Most of all, he had loved her.

'Did you have no idea?' she asked Richard as he stood gazing down in amazement at his sleeping twins. The babies were sharing the bassinet – there was only one of everything for the moment.

'No. Bateman never spotted it, I suppose. Sometimes it can be difficult, depending on what position the babies are lying in. Edith must have got a real surprise.' He gently stroked their heads.

'Well, *félicitations*, Richard. They are beautiful. Do you know what they are to be called?'

'Yes. We'd like to call the boy James, after Edith's father; that's what we'd decided if it was a boy. And Juliet, after my mother, if it was a girl. I suppose we will just use both.'

He was beaming but seemed hesitant, almost nervous, to pick them up.

'Go on,' she whispered.

'I'm afraid I'll wake them,' he replied.

Solange reached in and gathered the tiny babies up, placing one in each of his arms. They stirred and instantly fell back to sleep. Richard Buckley looked at his children and Solange saw raw emotion on his face for the first time since she'd known him. He gazed at their tiny faces and fingers, amazed at the miracle of life despite all his experience of death.

Eventually he spoke, 'Thank you, Solange, from the bottom of my heart, for delivering them safely and for taking care of them until Edith has had her rest.' He glanced at the bottle and tin of Nestlé powdered milk, still on the table. 'Poor girl, it must have been exhausting for her.'

'Of course,' she replied. 'I'm glad I was able to help. They are healthy little ones. They are enjoying the milk from the tins. I have never seen that before, but they are drinking it happily, so all is well.'

He said, clearly a little embarrassed, 'Well, to nurse twins would have been very difficult for her at first. I'm sure they will do wonderfully on the powdered milk for a day or two. I can't tell you how grateful I... *Edith* and I... are for all your help. Now, if you don't mind taking care of them for just a few more minutes, I've been in these clothes all night so I just need to clean up. I don't want to asphyxiate my children. I won't be long.'

'Of course.'

'Was that Dr Richard I heard?' Mrs Canty came bustling into the kitchen. Outside, the winter morning was brightening up at last. 'He must have been over the moon with the little beauties, God bless them. Anything from herself above? Is she interested in looking at her children? Not a bit of it, I suppose, and you up all night. Here give them to me and let you go for a snooze.'

Solange looked down at the two tiny babies, still in her arms from where Richard had handed them back to her. They slept soundly, their little fists bunched up tight. They were so pure, so innocent; they knew nothing of ugliness or brutality. For the first time since she had heard the news of Jeremy's death, she felt something thaw deep inside her.

All that morning, instead of sleeping as Richard and Mrs Canty insisted she must, she lay in bed thinking of the twins and hoping they were all right. When the quiet of the house was finally shattered by a newborn's cry, she couldn't stay in her room. She went downstairs to help Richard, who was attempting to feed one while the other bawled in the bassinet.

'Mrs Canty is just gone for a few messages; we need a few things from the shop. I told her I could manage but...' Richard was all fingers and thumbs.

As soon as Solange picked up and cuddled Juliet, she stopped crying. She started to suck on her bottle and began drifting off to sleep again. Then she did the same with James, and soon both babies were fast asleep.

'You have the magic touch with them, Solange,' Richard whispered in awe as they slept cuddled up together.

Gazing into the crib, she said, 'I think they like to be near each other. They have been close for all this time and now to be separated – it must be a shock.'

'MADAME?' SOLANGE TENTATIVELY ENTERED the bedroom, having first knocked gently on the door.

Edith was awake and propped up on pillows reading a letter that had arrived that morning.

'Yes, Solange? Did you want something?' she asked, still reading.

'I was wondering if you would like to see the babies. I could bring them to you.' She had contemplated simply walking into the room with the twins but had thought better of it.

'No, thank you, not just now. Are they well?' Edith asked as if enquiring about a distant relative.

'*Oui*, I mean, yes, Madame, they are very well and so beautiful.'

'Yes, I'm sure. I may come down to see them later. Although I'm sure they are better off not being disturbed from their routine.' Edith paused in her reading and looked up. 'Thank you for your assistance with the births. I am in your debt.' Her tone conveyed dismissal.

Still, Solange lingered. 'Madame, I am always happy to help.'

'Well, yes. It was good you were here.' Edith returned to her letter.

'And when you are ready for me to bring the babies to you...'

Edith looked up again with a sigh. 'Solange, not now, please. This is an important letter from an old friend of mine in Dublin. There are going to be changes in this country. Ireland may not remain the calm and peaceful place you imagine it to be. British imperialism will not be tolerated any longer. Now if you'll excuse me...'

This time, the implication that Solange was outstaying her welcome was too obvious to ignore.

Chapter 2

The weeks that followed were cold but bright. Solange wrapped up the babies well and took them for walks around the garden in their pram. The crocuses that bloomed in profusion around the trees delighted her. Her life had altered so irreparably and so often in these last months that she had lost all sense of continuity and this garden gave her an anchor to cling to in an ever-changing world. It was a comfort to know that spring had come again as it had always done, irrespective of the turmoil in human lives.

Yet the main distraction from her own sorrows came in caring for James and Juliet. She was deeply grateful that the endless demands of two such healthy infants gave her so little time to brood over all she had lost. The twins seemed never to sleep simultaneously and were always hungry. Richard insisted that it was not expected of her that she care for them, but given the continued lack of interest their mother showed in them, there seemed to be no other option.

He was so busy with the practice, and Mrs Canty, although a great help, had the household to run. Besides, Solange wanted to look after them. She could sit for hours just holding them and kissing their downy heads.

After Jeremy's death, she had moved as if in a trance. Presumably, she had slept and ate, but if so, she had no recollection of it. Life had stretched out in front of her as an endless, colourless void of time without him in it until she herself died. Over and over, she thought how things should have been different. He was a doctor, not even on the front line, yet he was dead. She thought of her Maman and Papa, too – so full of life and fun. Her mother's flashing eyes that could make her adoring husband agree to anything she wanted, and her father, who loved his sons and his only daughter with all his heart. But then Maman had got sick and died – a simple cut on her foot that had turned to blood poisoning. Papa was killed a short while later, shot by a German soldier in reprisal for some imagined slight. Her older brothers had fallen at Verdun, dying side by side as they had lived since early childhood. To be left entirely alone in the world was a terrifying prospect. Yet in those early weeks, all she had thought about was how she could manage to live without Jeremy.

She was by no means over her loss – she doubted she ever would be, but the twins had become her new reality, and she adored them more with each passing day.

Sometimes, she felt guilty for loving them as if she was their mother, yet Edith showed only the most cursory of interest in the babies. Once a day – or, on rare occasions, twice – she would descend into the kitchen to glance into their pram. She would enquire as to their health and whether they were eating or sleeping properly but without any sign of genuine concern. She never picked them up or even looked too closely at them. It really was as if Solange were their mother and Edith a gracious employer enquiring after her housemaid's children – something to be done as a matter of form, rather than stemming from any real desire to know.

Richard loved the twins and often gave them their bottles; occasionally he even changed a napkin – though not with much success. He asked daily if Edith had been down to see them, and if Solange thought that perhaps this was a question he should be putting to his wife, she gave no indication of it.

Time and again, Solange wondered how the Buckleys' marriage survived. Their union could not even be described as one of convenience; the entire household seemed to be a source of annoyance to Edith. Solange had long ceased to imagine that Edith's initial coldness to her had sprung from a natural caution; it was clear to her now that Edith's *ennui* extended to everyone in her life. Time and again, she witnessed Richard trying to get closer to his wife, but each time Edith rebuffed him – avoiding him whenever possible and engaging in brittle conversation with him only when it was necessary. The letters kept on coming – two, sometimes three, a week, from her friends in Dublin, all of whom were, it seemed, involved in the struggle for independence. It was the only subject on which Edith seemed close to animated and, perhaps because her husband showed no interest, she would often explain to Solange certain points regarding Irish politics.

Last week, Edith had summoned Solange to her room.

'Ah Solange, thank you for coming up. I think we need to talk, to clarify some things. Tell me, are you happy here?'

Solange was nonplussed. '*Oui*… I mean, yes, of course, Madame. I am very happy and grateful to you and Richard for…'

'No, I know that, but I think if you are happy to stay, we should formalise the arrangement. You are looking after the twins, no doubt admirably, and, therefore, we should be paying you. It is not reasonable of us to expect you to work for nothing. Now if you don't wish to do it, then of course there is no obligation on you; we will simply hire a nurse to come in. Please don't feel pressured due to some sense that you owe us something. That is simply not the case.'

Solange stood there wondering what to say. The thought of anyone else taking care of the babies was abhorrent to her; she loved them so much. Also, she had very little money. Jeremy was due a pension, but the process of claiming it was taking a very long time. She did need something to live on, but she wondered if Richard knew about this arrangement Edith was proposing. He was always so adamant that she was a member of the family.

'Well, Madame, I do love taking care of James and Juliet, so I am happy to do it. I don't know what else I would do if I did not do that. So yes, if it is acceptable to you and your husband then I would be glad of the job.'

'Good. That's settled then. Shall we say two hundred pounds per annum? And one and a half days off per week? Mrs Canty can cover your holidays. Of course, should you require more time off, please just ask, and we will arrange it. I think that's fair.'

Solange was impressed – she hadn't expected this cool, indifferent woman to be so generous. A nurse generally earned only one hundred pounds a year, and one day off per month was typical. 'That is most kind, Madame, but please deduct from that my board and lodging.'

'No. That won't be necessary. Ordinarily, that would be factored in, but these circumstances are far from typical. My husband promised your husband that we would be taking care of you and so we will. Now, there are some details we need to discuss.'

As part of her new role, Solange was to list all the items

necessary for the raising of two babies. She should not be thrifty, explained Edith – just simply write down whatever she thought they would require over the coming months, and Richard would see to it that everything was delivered. The babies were to be dressed exclusively from the Munster Arcade in Cork, or Arnott's in Dublin. Under no circumstances were they to be dressed in anything hand-knitted or bought locally. Prams and other paraphernalia were to come from Dublin also.

RICHARD SIGHED OVER HIS newspaper as he ate his breakfast in the kitchen with Solange and the twins.

'I never realised when I offered you a life of peace in Ireland, how things would turn out here. This struggle between the British and the IRA is, I fear, going to get worse. God knows how it will end.' He looked pensive but then seemed to shake himself out of it. 'Still, it's a bright spring morning and hopefully someone will get a bit of sense and end this before it escalates. Now, will we take this pair for a stroll before I face the parish and their ailments?'

He pushed one pram and Solange the other around the path that encircled the house. The April sun warmed the old walls of Dunderrig and the garden had sprung to life. At nearly four months, the twins were thriving and loved to lie without blankets and furiously kick their chubby legs.

'They are so beautiful, *n'est-ce pas*?' Solange smiled. 'I don't know much about this independence war, I don't read the papers though I should I suppose, but it just all seems so…'

'Pointless? Repetitive? Futile?' Richard suggested.

She nodded. 'After France and everything that we saw, war seems to be just waste. Nothing else, just waste. People, property, land, villages. I hope this is not the same fate for your home, Richard.'

Their relationship had become less formal in the past

months. Richard would always be reticent, and she spoke as guardedly as he, but they enjoyed a good relationship. He was becoming more accustomed to fatherhood and was taking more and more of an active role in the care of his children. He'd even mastered changing their napkins. Nothing had improved with their mother though she did still visit the kitchen once a day to glance briefly at them.

THE TWINS WERE BAPTISED in the local Catholic parish church and on the morning of the christening, Edith arrived downstairs looking so glamorous that she took Solange's breath away. She had only seen the doctor's wife in nightgowns up to then and was amazed to see how elegant Edith could be with her hair pinned in an elegant chignon and wearing a beautifully tailored dress, cut daringly low at both front and back, with panels of cream sat alongside panels of ivory and white. Solange had never seen anything like it on a real person before, but she had taken to looking over various fashion magazines when Edith had finished with them. So she knew that since the war, when women had learnt to drive cars and wear trousers, they were reluctant to incarcerate themselves once more in torturous corsets and restrictive dresses. The postwar generation was raising hemlines and dropping necklines and, despite living in West Cork, it seemed Edith Buckley was not going to be left behind. For the first time, Solange could see why Richard had married her. She was so beautiful.

The twins were also dressed handsomely – Juliet in the simple christening robe that had been used to baptise at least four generations of Buckleys, and James in an identical robe made for the occasion by Mrs Canty. Both babies were wrapped in elaborately embroidered white blankets.

Mrs Canty told Solange she had overheard Richard and Edith arguing about the christening robes. Edith had wanted to order new ones from some French couturier based in

Dublin but for once Richard had put his foot down. Every Buckley baby was baptised in the family gown and the twins were not going to be an exception. Mrs Canty delighted in telling the tale of how 'The One' – as Edith was unflatteringly called by her – got her comeuppance.

Richard made two trips in the car that day: the first, bringing Mrs Canty and her husband and a silent Edith to the church; the next, to collect Solange and the twins. As Solange entered the church with a baby in each arm, she felt the eyes of at least a hundred people upon her. Perhaps she imagined it, but it seemed as if they were more interested in her than in the babies. Edith and Richard sat side by side in the front pew, not touching, and next to them sat Dr Bateman and his wife, who were standing as the children's godparents. Once again, Solange was struck by the peculiar ways of the Irish. These people were offering to be the babies' guardians in the event of their parents' death, yet here in the church on the morning of their christening was the first time they had ever even seen them.

Dr Bateman had called late on the morning of the birth to ensure Edith was well and that she had delivered safely. He had complimented Solange on her professionalism and when she had asked if he'd like to examine the babies, he had stated that he was quite sure they were in excellent hands between her and their father, and promptly left. He had not appeared in Dunderrig since.

The babies were duly baptised and afterwards Richard invited a select group of people – friends and family, Solange assumed – to the Eldon Hotel in Skibbereen for lunch. He'd pleaded with her the night before to come to the lunch, but she had refused. Edith wouldn't want her there – she was staff now, whether Richard liked it or not, and it wouldn't have been appropriate.

Chapter 3

*R*ichard sat beside the fire in his study thinking about his wife. She had been bored and disparaging ever since her arrival at Dunderrig. He had hoped that the twins would soften her heart, but it hadn't happened. He tried to pinpoint the time when she had turned into this cold, snobbish person.

She had been such a beautiful, quiet, serene kind of girl. Such a restful person to be around, that he had decided only two weeks after meeting her at that hospital dance in England that she was the girl for him. He wasn't much of a dancer, but Jeremy had convinced him to have a night out. They had almost finished their training in Beauford Hospital, in Bristol, and Jeremy was planning to join up as soon as he qualified. There was a girl that Jeremy had had his eye on all week, and he was determined to have a crack at her. Richard was used to his friend falling for a new girl every few days; he also knew Jeremy would not let him rest until he agreed to accompany him to the dance. It was easier just to give in.

Richard had never had much success with girls. He had always envisaged himself married, but the process of becoming so seemed a bit of a mystery. There were a few girls at home in Dunderrig who were chatty and seemed friendly, but he was painfully shy and clammed up whenever a girl approached him. Since meeting Jeremy, it had become even harder for him to meet anyone – the girls were always dazzled by his handsome and vivacious friend while he himself faded into the background.

He had seen Edith straight away when he walked in. He had plucked up the courage to speak to her after he heard her ordering a cup of tea in an Irish accent. She had been visiting an elderly relative in Bristol and had been convinced to attend the dance by her cousin. They danced several times that night, and Richard was sure he had never seen a girl as beautiful. They had gone to tea the following day and for a walk afterwards. She seemed to be happy to discuss issues of the day but rarely answered a direct question and made very few demands on him emotionally; often they just strolled in comfortable silence.

Yet on their fifth date as they walked through the Clifton area of Bristol, he had inquired about her parents. And after some hesitation, she had told him that her mother had died when she was still a child and that her father had become everything to her. Then, after much prompting, she told him her father's story. He had been a professor of English and History in University College Dublin, who regularly spoke out against the horrendous living conditions endured by the working classes. He had supported Jim Larkin in encouraging the workers' strike of 1913 and had been addressing a rally when a riot erupted between the crowd and the police. Badly injured in the ensuing melee, he had died a week later of his wounds.

The normally serene Edith became visibly upset as she spoke, and he realised then how difficult it was for her to discuss such emotional issues. There had been minimal physical contact between them up to that point but there, in the middle of the street, he had held her in his arms and comforted her. That was the turning point; she was so vulnerable and beautiful, and he decided he wanted to take care of her, always.

After that initial fortnight in Bristol, they arranged to stay in touch when Edith returned to Dublin. He was working hard in the hospital, gaining experience before deciding his next move. He'd always intended returning to Dunderrig and taking over the practice from his father, but the old doctor wasn't yet ready to retire, and besides, meeting Edith had made him rethink. She seemed very settled in Dublin and so, after a few months of letters and an occasional meeting, he had accepted a locum position in Kingstown. Edith had been so pleased. He had proposed in Stephen's Green, and she had agreed happily. He smiled ruefully at the memory. Nothing he did seemed to please her these days.

Those days in Dublin seemed a lifetime ago now. Edith had been happy and busy then; she had continued her interest in matters political, and he was so absorbed in his work that he was only glad she had a wide circle of friends to keep her occupied. Many of them were well-known literary and political figures – people who had known her father. Occasionally, they came to the house for dinner or drinks; yet while Richard did his best, he found their conversation about the Irish cause a little wearisome. It wasn't that he didn't care, but these academics and writers seemed so far removed from the common people they purported to represent. He contributed very little to these conversations, and he knew his lack of enthusiasm embarrassed Edith. They never argued, but he remembered one such dinner at a grand house in Ballsbridge when he'd explained to an artist sitting on his left that while Irish independence was of course something to aspire to, it wasn't worth one drop of blood. He said that negotiation and dialogue were the only way and that he hoped a peaceful solution could be found.

He would never forget the looks from their fellow diners; it was as if he'd just said something incredibly rude or vulgar. Edith was furious with him and didn't speak to him all the way home. From then on, he didn't attend those dinners – much to the relief of them both. They rubbed along well together, while not seeing too much of each other.

And that was where everything would have stayed, had he not received that letter from Jeremy describing the conditions in the hospital in Amiens. It was not in the true Jeremy style – his letters were usually about his passion for the gorgeous Solange. Before he'd convinced her to marry him, he had regularly asked Richard's opinion about how to get her to see him as someone serious, rather than a playboy. Richard found the idea of Jeremy asking *him* for advice ridiculous. Jeremy was the one who could talk to women. He himself could barely manage a romantic relationship with his own wife.

This latest letter was in a different vein, however, as Jeremy described the kind of injuries the young men at the front were sustaining and how supplies and staffing levels were woefully inadequate. He wrote of the horrors suffered by so many Irishmen in the bloodbath of the Somme – many of them from the Munster Fusiliers regiment, from Richard's native west Cork. Suddenly, the idea of going to France, making a difference and helping his own countrymen seemed the logical thing to do. He asked his parents if Edith could live with them in Dunderrig while he was in France, and they agreed at once. The idea that his wife would refuse never crossed his mind.

'No,' she said calmly when he had finished.

'No? No to what? To Dunderrig? Look, Edith, I know you have your friends here, but I can't leave you here alone and unprotected.'

'It's true that I do not want to go to Dunderrig. My life is here. I am helping, doing something worthwhile, something my father would be proud of. But nor do I want you putting on a British uniform and fighting for their King.' She spoke slowly but with steeliness to her tone he had never heard before.

'But Edith, my dear, I won't be fighting. I'm a doctor. I will be working in a hospital, tending to the wounded. I don't have any political opinions about it; I simply want to help. Irish boys are out there too, you know, thousands of them. Please try to understand, I love you, but I have to go. And while I'm gone, I want you to be safe.' He was aware he was pleading.

She looked as if she was weighing up whether or not to continue. Her voice held a bitterness he'd never heard from her before. 'Yes, Richard. There are thousands of Irishmen fighting. Thousands of traitors to their own country. If they were so anxious to fight for something, then why not here, on their own soil, for their own people? You know how I feel about the British, and everything they stand for. Their puppet police murdered my father. Murdered him, Richard, for having the courage to speak out. I cannot support you putting that uniform on your back. Frankly, I'm shocked that you would even consider it. The Rising might have ended in disaster, but we are not beaten. Already we are working on getting our men out of British gaols and when they come home, I want to be here, in Dublin. *Here* is where you should be, looking after your own, not risking your life and wasting your skills in a country that has nothing to do with us. I am asking you, as your wife, not to do this.'

Richard felt as if he were seeing her for the first time – he had been so busy with the practice, he hadn't realised how deeply she had become involved with the volunteers. Since the Rising the previous Easter, the city had been on tenterhooks. It seemed to him now that her support of an Irish republic could only get her into trouble, and that it was more important than ever that she relocate to the peaceful backwater of Dunderrig while he was away in France and unable to protect her.

At first, he tried to reason with her, 'Edith, I do understand your loyalty to your father. He was an honourable and brave man, but really, this is no environment for a woman, let alone one whose husband is away. I love you, and I want you to be safe. Please try to understand my reasons for going. I don't agree with war – I hate it, in fact – but medicine is not about ideology. The boys and men who are suffering need me to help them. I'm sorry you are unhappy, but I must insist that you go to Dunderrig. I would be out of my mind with worry were you to stay here.'

She looked at him with disgust, and from that moment on, she rebuffed all efforts he made to be conciliatory. They had driven to Dunderrig in silence a few weeks later and everything he said was greeted with monosyllabic responses. His parents went to great lengths to make their daughter-in-law welcome, yet Edith showed them the same level of disdain she now did Richard. His father had taken him aside and questioned him what was the matter, whether they had done something wrong. Richard didn't wish to explain. He simply said that Edith would need to get used to country living, and that would take time; he was sure they would be a comfort to Edith, and she to them. Then, with a heavy heart, he set sail for England.

FOR RICHARD, THE WAR passed in a haze of noise and blood. There was nothing glorious or noble about it, just the daily and nightly grind of trying to patch together the broken bodies with which he was constantly presented. He tried to get home on leave to see Edith, but he'd only managed it twice. He wrote long letters, but she replied only with short notes – answering all questions he asked her but with absolutely no warmth. Still, she had met with unexpected enthusiasm the news that he was coming home on leave in May of 1918 and announced she was coming to Dublin to meet him off the boat. He half-suspected his wife was more interested in seeing Dublin than in seeing him. He had heard from his mother that she often travelled up to the city, staying with friends overnight. He supposed there was no harm in it. It must be dull for a young woman to be stuck in a house with his elderly parents and no one her own age to befriend. He knew some of his old school friends' wives had made efforts to include her in their social circle, but it seemed she was still very much a Dublin girl. He told himself that when he returned home and the war was over, they would patch up their marriage, hopefully have children, and all would be well. By then, she would have forgiven him.

They arranged to meet at the Bayview Hotel in Kingstown. They had often gone there for dinner in the early days of their marriage, so he hoped the location would rekindle their love. When Richard arrived at the hotel, around seven in the evening, he had expected to find her dressed for a night out. Instead, he was surprised to be greeted by his wife wearing a negligee and even more delighted to find her in an amorous mood. They'd made love quickly and silently. Richard would have liked to remain in bed with her, but she was determined that they go down to dinner. She never asked about his life in France. A group of her friends were waiting for them in the dining room. Hiding his disappointment, he made light conversation; his wife had taken up smoking and kept abandoning him for the terrace of the seafront hotel. Yet he was so happy to see her animated and smiling again that he indulged her and agreed to her suggestion that they stay in the hotel for a few more days before travelling to Dunderrig. Although his leave was suddenly cut short before he could get home to see his parents, he had returned to France with a lighter heart. In her next, very short letter, she had told him she was pregnant. He was overjoyed, although worried that she expressed no pleasure in the news.

THE DEATHS OF HIS parents from influenza came as a shocking blow to him. It happened only weeks after he'd been in Ireland, and he was crushed not just by grief but also by guilt that he had been in the country but hadn't managed to travel down to Dunderrig to see them. If only he hadn't agreed to stay those extra days in Kingstown. He wrote long letters to Edith, describing his pain as best he could but, while she commiserated, he could tell that the death of the old couple meant much more to their housekeeper Mrs Canty and her husband Eddie than to his own wife. He longed to go home but could not get leave. John and Juliet Buckley were buried in the cemetery in the village without their only child there to say goodbye.

As the war wore on wearyingly to its end, the waves of wounded growing daily, Richard received a second, longer letter from Edith:

Dear Richard,

I hope you are well and that you will be home safely before too long. The house is very quiet without your parents though Mrs Canty does her best to fill it with her relentless prattle. I am well though I have been feeling quite nauseous. Mrs Canty's boiling of cabbage does little to help that situation. I have not been up to Dublin in some time, so I have no news about anything there. I am under the care of Dr Bateman from Cork. The child will be born in January sometime, he thinks. I hope you will have returned by then. I know we have had our differences, Richard, but now that we are to be parents I think we should make the best of it for the sake of our child.

Fond regards,

Your wife,

Edith.

Richard felt great relief. *Fond regards.* Impending motherhood had clearly softened her. The war was in its final stages, he was sure of it, and he would return to Dunderrig, take over the practice and raise his family with Edith. Everything would be all right.

To read on please visit this link:

So Much Owed

ABOUT THE AUTHOR

Jean Grainger is a USA Today bestselling Irish author. She writes historical and contemporary Irish fiction and her work has very flatteringly been compared to the late great Maeve Binchy.

She lives in a stone cottage in Cork with her husband Diarmuid and the youngest two of her four children. The older two come home for a break when adulting gets too exhausting. There are a variety of animals there too, all led by two cute but clueless micro-dogs called Scrappy and Scoobi.

ALSO BY JEAN GRAINGER

The Tour Series

The Tour

Safe at the Edge of the World

The Story of Grenville King

The Homecoming of Bubbles O'Leary

Finding Billie Romano

Kayla's Trick

The Carmel Sheehan Story

Letters of Freedom

The Future's Not Ours To See

What Will Be

The Robinswood Story

What Once Was True

Return To Robinswood

Trials and Tribulations

The Star and the Shamrock Series

The Star and the Shamrock

The Emerald Horizon

The Hard Way Home

The World Starts Anew

The Queenstown Series

Last Port of Call

The West's Awake

The Harp and the Rose

Roaring Liberty

Standalone Books

So Much Owed

Shadow of a Century

Under Heaven's Shining Stars

Catriona's War

Sisters of the Southern Cross

The Kilteegan Bridge Series

The Trouble with Secrets

What Divides Us

More Harm Than Good

When Irish Eyes Are Lying

A Silent Understanding

The Mags Munroe Story

The Existential Worries of Mags Munroe

Growing Wild in the Shade

Each to their Own

Cullens Celtic Cabaret

For All The World

A Beautiful Ferocity

Rivers of Wrath - coming November 2023

Made in United States
Cleveland, OH
12 February 2025

14308367R00090